CW01584432

Confessions of a Massage Madam, Sharon.

BIANCA THOMAS

authorHOUSE®

AuthorHouse™ UK
1663 Liberty Drive
Bloomington, IN 47403 USA
www.authorhouse.co.uk
Phone: UK TFN: 0800 0148641 (Toll Free inside the UK)
UK Local: 02036 956322 (+44 20 3695 6322 from outside the UK)

© 2021 Bianca Thomas. All rights reserved.

No part of this book may be reproduced, stored in a retrieval system, or transmitted by any means without the written permission of the author.

Published by AuthorHouse 06/22/2021

ISBN: 978-1-6655-9066-2 (sc)
ISBN: 978-1-6655-9065-5 (hc)
ISBN: 978-1-6655-9064-8 (e)

Print information available on the last page.

Any people depicted in stock imagery provided by Getty Images are models, and such images are being used for illustrative purposes only.
Certain stock imagery © Getty Images.

This book is printed on acid-free paper.

Because of the dynamic nature of the Internet, any web addresses or links contained in this book may have changed since publication and may no longer be valid. The views expressed in this work are solely those of the author and do not necessarily reflect the views of the publisher, and the publisher hereby disclaims any responsibility for them.

This book is based on true accounts of what actually happens in a massage parlour. Madam Sharon wrote it from true events. The explicit sexual activities of *Fifty Shades of Grey* have nothing on this story; it's a very exciting read for those interested in verbal sex.

AS THE PRISON DOOR SLAMMED loudly behind her, she stood there with tears in her eyes, feeling demoralised at the way she had been treated when she entered the prison. When Sharon arrived there, she had been taken handcuffed into the reception, where there were several girls lying around on sofas. Some were sleeping, and some were just staring into space. A couple of girls had been thrown out of the toilets for smoking. At first, Sharon thought they had just arrived after a long journey, but it turned out they were high on drugs and spaced out.

Sharon sat around waiting for a long time—hours. Finally, she was taken to a cubicle and searched all over. Her personal belongings were taken away from her, and she was given some toiletries. At that moment, she got the feeling, *I'm not in control of my life.*

The prison cell was about six by ten feet. She looked around to survey the cell; it had a small barred window looking out to fields. This was a country prison. The room had a single bed by the wall, and at the foot of the bed was a long cupboard reaching to the door, which had a window so they could spy on her. On the opposite wall, there was a desk with an electric kettle and a cupboard above for her cup and plate.

Sharon was a tall person, age 52, with dark brown hair halfway down her back. She was quite slim with very large breasts. She was a rather attractive lady with a slight cockney accent, as she had lived in London for part of her life. She had an unhealthy interest in men.

Men were always taking advantage of her. When she was about 11 years old, she was walking past a pub one evening when some men came out. One of the men was called Paddy Maginty. She innocently said hello to him; he grabbed hold of her face and snogged her. As he did so, she could feel the rough, prickly stubble of his unshaven face.

The poor girl was horrified. Since that incident, she had never been able to feel a man's stubbled face without thinking of Paddy Maginty. It had always haunted her.

Sharon was born in Barking in Essex and grew up in Essex. Her parents owned a grocery shop. They were very hard-working people who worked seven days a week. Also when Sharon was 11 years old, her parents sold the grocery shop and moved down to Harwich.

Harwich was a small town with a dock. Ships went from there to Holland and Sweden. Just across the water from Harwich, there was a naval base where the young sailors were trained. They were all from the HMS *Ganges.*

Although Harwich was a small town, it was busy when the *Ganges* hit the town a couple of nights a week. Also, when the ships came in from Holland, the seamen came ashore and frequented the many pubs. There were about eighteen pubs in this very small town, and they were almost next door to one another. Harwich had a pleasant beach and an area called a *quay* where youngsters hung out. In the late fifties, you could go across to another port called Felixstowe for the price of one shilling and six pence. The trip took about fifty-five minutes. Harwich also had a ferry that ferried trains to Holland. They did have weekend trips to Sweden for a dirty weekend.

Sharon's parents rented a large shop with a flat. The flat had about eight rooms. It was on two floors. It also had a large cellar. The building was on a corner of two roads: Market Street and Church Street. The shop was very dirty. It was a chemist in its former life, and it was filled with hundreds of old medicine bottles of all shapes and sizes. There was so much dust on them, as they had been locked away for maybe ten years or more. All the family helped out, including Sharon and her two brothers, Ivan and Steve.

Soon, the place was cleaned up, and Sharon's parents decided to open the shop as a cafe. Sharon's dad, Jack, thought it would be a good idea to put a television in it and call it the Tellytubby Cafe. As there were plenty of rooms upstairs, the family was able to do a bed-and-breakfast.

Sharon and her brothers joined school and soon settled into their new lives in the new town. When the cafe opened, it became quite busy. It had a jukebox, and the teenagers would come in and listen to their favourite music. This cafe was an asset to the town. At night, the seamen would come in and order hamburgers and hot dogs. The pubs closed at half past ten in those days, so the guys would come into the cafe to eat after a night of drinking.

There were quite a few young girls in the town. On the nights the HMS *Ganges* came to town, the girls would appear all tarted up to attract the guys. They would trot around in four-to six-inch stiletto shoes, very tight pencil skirts, and very revealing tops to accentuate their very large breasts. If they didn't have large breasts, they would wear padded bras to make it look as though they did have large breasts. In those days, nylons were in fashion. Some had seams going all the way up the backs of the girls' legs, and some were plain. They had to be held up by suspender belts and suspenders. The men liked the nylons; they really were a turn-on for them.

THE GIRLS IN THE TOWN couldn't wait for the seamen to come ashore. Some of the girls were only 13 years old, but they looked so grown-up the sailors thought they were about 19. That was OK as long as they didn't get pregnant. There was no such thing as the pill in those days, and AIDS was certainly unheard of, so apart from VD—which was bad enough—pregnancy was the only concern. They all had a good time. A few girls probably did get pregnant. There are probably plenty of people around Harwich who don't know their dads.

Sharon never went out at night dressed up like the other girls. Her mother wouldn't let her; she was only twelve. She helped out in the cafe. She liked the cafe because she enjoyed getting to know the customers. At night, after a while, the television was turned off, and the jukebox would be playing. It was equipped with all the top-twenty records, which played all evening. Harwich only got one radio station which played rock and roll music, and that was Radio Luxembourg. The problem with that was the signal was very poor; it was almost impossible to hear it. So the teenagers enjoyed going to the cafe to listen to records.

Sharon's mother, Joan, cleared out what was a storeroom and made it into a room for the teenagers to dance. The jukebox was fitted with speakers so they could hear it in the back room and jive to the music. The most popular singers were Elvis Presley, Cliff Richard, Marty Wilde, Billy Fury, Paul Anka, Connie Francis, Brenda Lee, and Shirley Bassey. All the youngsters had a whale of a time in the Tellytubby Cafe, and Sharon enjoyed it too. Sharon was a very well-developed girl for twelve. She was already wearing a size-38 bra. She was also tall and slender.

Because the cafe had a lot of bedrooms, Joan rented out the

bedrooms for ten shillings a night. It was convenient for the seamen because sometimes, the guys would get stranded ashore if they missed the last tug back to their ship, which would be anchored just off shore. So they would get a bed for the night. One night, Sharon went to bed early, and around eleven o'clock, she got up and went downstairs to get a drink of water when she met a seaman on the stairs. He stopped her and started chatting to her and asked her to show him round the town on Saturday. He wouldn't take no for an answer. So she had to agree just to get past him.

When he told Joan he was going to take her daughter out on Saturday, Joan said,

'No, you're not; she's only twelve.' Well, the guy was absolutely shocked.

Sometime later, three Irish guys came to Harwich to run a pipeline from Harwich to Birmingham. They needed somewhere to stay for three months, so they stayed at the cafe. One of the guys was named Michael. He was fair-haired with blue eyes and was six feet, six inches tall.

One evening, when Sharon was going down the stairs, she met Michael, and they had a chat. Then as they were chatting, Michael got hold of Sharon's hands, held them tightly behind her back, and kissed her on the mouth. He put his mouth over hers and sucked her mouth into his. It was warm, moist, and soft just like a marshmallow. Although Sharon was only 12, being kissed really excited her. It was strong and hot, and it made her tingle. She had never felt anything like that before. It was as though all her energy had drained from her. She liked it and hoped he would kiss her again. When she went back upstairs, she felt quite flushed. Still tingly. She never told anyone about it; she kept it to herself. After that, every time she met Michael on the stairs, he would kiss her. Sometimes, she would keep a lookout for him so he could do it again.

Michael was starting to get feelings for this girl, so he asked Joan if he could take Sharon to the pictures. Joan said, 'She's only 12.' Michael said he would behave himself and look after her. So Joan said, 'As long as you promise to behave, she can go.' So Sharon got dressed up in a straight skirt and high heels. Actually, they were Joan's; she borrowed them because she didn't want to look like a school girl when going to the pictures with such a tall man. Michael was twenty-one.

Michael paid for the seats in the back row. *The Bridge on the River Kwai* was showing, not that she got to see any of it. Michael kissed her all the way through the film. He kept trying to touch her between her thighs, but Sharon wasn't having any of that; she was quite scared. She felt invaded of her privacy. Although she was quite turned on, she was embarrassed. She had never shown anyone her vagina before, let alone let them touch it. No, she wasn't ready for that yet.

After that date, Sharon felt that Michael was her boyfriend. In the evenings, when she helped out in the cafe, Michael would stay near the counter with her while she was serving the customers.

One night, the cafe closed at about 10:30, and they were on their own. They went into the back of the cafe and started kissing again. While they were kissing, Michael undid his fly, took out his very erect penis, and put it into her hand. This was the very first time she had seen or felt something so big and firm, yet at the same time, the skin felt so soft to touch. She didn't quite know what to do with it at first. So she caressed it for a few minutes, and it got harder and harder.

Michael seemed to be getting very passionate. Then suddenly, he let out a loud gasp, and sperm started spurting out of his penis. Then everything was calm. *Wah wah wah.* Just a few minutes later, Sharon's stepfather appeared in the doorway and demanded to know what was going on. Sharon was sent straight to bed.

Many years later, after two failed marriages and two now-grown-up children, Sharon decided to move to London and open an aromatherapy clinic. She rented a two-bedroom flat above some shops in Neasden in North London. She moved in very late on a Sunday night, so that night, she didn't unpack any boxes. They lay all over the lounge.

Eight o'clock the next morning, the phone rang, and a man's voice over the phone said, 'I know you will find this hard to believe, but I have a problem in my groin. You see, I have a blocked lymph gland, and I need it to be massaged regularly— about twice a week—as my leg could get very swollen.'

As Sharon had studied physiology and anatomy, she knew what he was talking about. He said it was urgent—that he needed to come along right now. Sharon said, 'I haven't even unpacked my boxes yet.'

He said, 'Don't worry about that.'

So Sharon thought for a minute, then said, 'You can come along now, but I warn you: the place is in a mess.'

He said, 'That doesn't matter.'

Sharon set up the massage table and prepared the massage oils, cleaned the massage table with antibacterial cleaner and covered it with clean white towels, and put on her white therapist's coat, ready to let the man in. About twenty minutes later, the man arrived, and she opened the door for him. He was a tall, slim man in his middle sixties. He was dressed in a grey polo shirt, navy shorts, and a pair of Jesus sandals with socks about three-quarters of the way up his legs. She showed him into the lounge and asked him to remove his clothes and lie on the massage table while she went into the bathroom to wash her hands.

He asked, 'Shall I remove my pants?'

Sharon said, 'It'd be a job to massage your groin with them on.'

So he took everything off and was sitting bolt upright when Sharon re-entered the room. Sharon rubbed massage oil into her hands and warned him her hands might feel a little cold. He said, 'That's fine.'

She started quite gently at first to get him used to the cold hands. She massaged at the side of the knee and gradually along the inside of the leg in circular movements, gradually working up to his groin as to elevate the blockage. As she was doing this, he started to get aroused. He apologised for this. She was very understanding and said to relax.

After she had finished the treatment, she asked him if he wanted hand relief. He said, 'Yes, please.' So she massaged his penis until he ejaculated. Then he got dressed and gave her £10 extra. She was very pleased with this, so she thought she would offer this relief to all her clients and include it in the price. So that was the beginning of the naughty massage parlour, which later became an agreed-on brothel.

Sharon started to get very busy. She was doing about seven massages a day, so she decided to employ a cleaner. A black woman named Margaret applied for the job, and Sharon offered her £8 per hour, mainly to clean the stairs, as her place was on the second floor. Sharon liked Margaret straight away. She was in her fifties, and she was a character. She reminded Sharon of Whoopi Goldberg. After she had worked there for a few weeks, Sharon said to her, 'How would you like to learn to do massage? Then you can earn some decent money.' Margaret agreed.

So Sharon had to get somebody to be a model for training Margaret. She knew a guy named Simon. Simon was an eccentric type of person. He lived on his own, he was about 35 years old, and he had an Indian appearance, though he spoke with a North London accent. He dressed in a dark, long jacket with a hood and always carried a large holdall in his hands. He always looked as though he was going somewhere. He had a gentle demeanour. He was slim and petite and was easy to massage. When Sharon asked him if he would like to be a model for her, he was delighted. So he was always available.

Sharon told Margaret it was important to learn to massage properly. Massage wasn't a quick run up and down the body and then naughty stuff. It was important to get the client completely relaxed and in a state of trance before the sexual activity. Then the client would be putty in your hands. So Margaret had massage lessons every day for about a week. It was crucial that she understand what she was doing and the importance of it. Margaret was a very good student, and Simon was so relaxed he thought he was on a health farm.

ONCE MARGARET HAD LEARNT HOW to massage, Sharon was able to pass on some customers to her. Margaret took to it like a duck in water. Very soon, clients were requesting her and frequently returned. There were plenty of clients for both of the women. Sometimes, clients would ask to have the two massage ladies together so they could experience having four hands on them at the same time. And if the girls wanted to take their tops off, they could have four breasts on them also, sliding all along their backs, which were covered with massage oil. It was very erotic. Also, some guys would be excited by the fact that one woman was black and the other white. Sharon and Margaret made a very good team.

Margaret had a very tall, very pale client with ginger hair. He was a credit controller. He came to see Margaret a couple of times a week and seemed quite attracted to her. One night, he asked her to go out on a date with him. The next day, when she arrived for work, she complained to Sharon that he didn't have a car and that she had never been on a date on a train before.

This guy wasn't taking no for an answer; he kept pursuing her. It turned out that he was very rich. After a few months, he married her, and they bought a very nice house, and he bought her a very nice car and taught her to drive. Margaret left Sharon and enjoyed her new married life, having transitioned from working as a cleaning lady to marrying a very nice rich man in just a few months. Sharon and she kept in touch.

Sharon now had to find a new massage lady. She was back on her own again.

One day while Sharon was massaging a client, the phone rang, and she answered it. A very bubbly girl on the other end of the phone asked Sharon if she knew what aloe vera was. Sharon replied, 'Yes, it is fluid from a plant a bit like a cactus plant, and it has good healing properties and is very good for damaged skin.' The girl then asked if she could make an appointment to come along and get Sharon some aloe vera. So Sharon made an appointment for the following week.

When the girl, whose name was Sally, arrived, Sharon invited her in and offered her a cup of coffee. Sally meanwhile got out her aloe vera brochures and started showing Sharon what was on offer. Sharon gave her an order for the skincare products, and Sally put the order in her book.

Sally was a very attractive lady with very large breasts and very long, curly black hair. Sharon said to her, 'You are a very attractive woman. And with a body like yours, I don't know what you earn in a month, but whatever it is, you could earn more in a week than you do in a month if you came and worked for me.'

SALLY SAID SHE COULDN'T DO that; her father would kill her. Sharon told her she was to think about it. They had another cup of coffee, and Sally left.

The following week, the aloe vera turned up. And a few days later, Sally phoned and said she would like to take Sharon up on her offer. Sharon was delighted, as she was getting worn out from trying to do all the work by herself. She promptly got on the phone to her model, Simon, and asked him to come round the following day; he was more than happy to oblige.

The next day, a lovely Tuesday in November, the sun was shining. It's not often you get a sunny morning in November. Sharon was up early. She had to tell her clients not to come before lunchtime, as she was going to be busy in the morning training a beautiful new girl. They were intrigued. They said, 'This one isn't going to run off and get married, is she?'

At 10:30, the doorbell rang, and Sally was at the door, looking very nervous. Sharon asked her in and told her, 'Don't be nervous. It will be fun, and nobody is going to make you do anything you don't want to do.' Sharon introduced Sally to Simon, who had arrived early, and they all sat down and had a cup of coffee. While they were having their coffee, Sharon took the opportunity to explain the protocol with the clients, the massage pricing, and how much Sally had to pay for using the massage room and the supplies, such as the couch roll, the massage oils, hot water, and towels. She and Sally agreed on the price of use of the massage room and supplies: £20 per client.

Then Simon undressed and lay on the massage table, and Sharon started the first lesson in massage. She spent a couple of hours showing

Sally all the moves and explained the reasons for each move as she went along. Sally's training took a couple of hours each day for five days. Sharon insisted she learn properly. Sharon was the best, and anyone who worked for her had to be the best. Although Sharon didn't have the diplomas for teaching, she did have the skills, and the clients wouldn't accept anything less. They were spoiled, but Sharon was too busy to attend to all of them.

Sally was very taken with the massage lessons; she learnt quickly and was looking forward to starting work. When Sharon felt Sally was ready to begin working with clients, Sharon changed Sally's name to Lola. For her first week of work, Lola got her children set up with a caretaker. She and Sharon had agreed that she would work only weekday hours because she wanted to be at home with her children on weekends. That was fine with Sharon.

On Monday morning—her first day of work—Lola turned up at ten o'clock. That was the time Sharon started work. Lola would work from ten to six. When the clients knew a new girl was starting, they were very anxious to have a massage with her. In fact, most of them wanted to try out the new girl. Sharon was beginning to think she would lose all her clients to Lola. Still, the money would be coming in, and she needed to rest for a bit; she had been working seven days a week from early morning to late at night.

After a few weeks, once the clients were used to Lola, some of them asked if they could have a two-girl massage, with Sharon and Lola massaging them at the same time. They were quite prepared to pay double, although in actual fact, they would pay £20 less than double because the room was already paid for.

One guy, an Indian named Ali, wanted the two girls to be wearing only their panties. So all his massages started with the back, with him lying face down. One girl would start with both her hands on his bum, cover him with massage oil, and firmly glide her hands up his back to his shoulders. And while she was doing that, her naked, warm breasts would be gently touching his bare skin, down his arms to his elbows, then back up his arms, round his neck, and back down his back to the base of his bum. She would do that several times. While she was doing that, the other girl would be moving her hands from the bottom of one foot all the way up the back of one of his legs and round his bum and back several times. While she was doing that, as her hand rotated round the cheeks of his bum, he would raise his bum in the air, sort of inviting her to massage it more accurately and cover more of the erogenous zones around that area. She would be doing one leg at a time.

The back and leg massage would take around half an hour. Once that was done, the guy would have to turn over for the front to be done, which would also take a half an hour. While all of this was going on for the first time, Ali got an erection. He got very excited lying there, having two semi-naked women massage his body. His erection went up and down all the time, his penis moving from side to side all by itself. Ali tried to touch the girls, but they had none of that. They told him that if he didn't keep still, he was going to be spanked. That only aroused him more, so by then, Lola had to take his very erect penis in her hand and shake it with a very firm touch to relieve him. He quickly ejaculated and closed his eyes in relaxation. He said he thought he'd died and gone to heaven. This was an electric experience; he'd never felt anything like this before, and he was definitely coming back next week.

As time went by, the massage parlour got busier and busier. Lola seemed to be enjoying her work. Some days, she would spend two hours with the same client, and when she came out of the room, she would be quite red and hot in the face. Sharon never asked her what she had been up to. As long as Sharon got paid for the amount of time Sally was in the room, which would be £40 for two hours, that was all she cared about.

At weekends, the parlour was mostly closed, as Lola only worked weekdays and Sharon would go away to her country cottage with her boyfriend. One day, Lola said to Sharon, 'I know a couple of ladies who would like to work here weekends.' It suited them because they both had jobs to go to during the week. Sharon thought about it and said to herself, *It can't do any harm. Let's do it.*

The following weekend, the two women turned up. One was named Paulene. She was about forty-five and blonde and worked in a solicitor's office. And the other one was a receptionist named Sandy. She was about thirty-five and a brunette. Sharon showed the women where everything was: towels, oils, couch roll, and other stuff, like tea and coffee. And she left the key for them and told them to leave the money in the safe for the use of the rooms: £20 for each client. What they didn't know was there was a CCTV camera in the room.

When Sharon got back on Monday morning, the first thing she did was check the CCTV. After a few minutes of waiting, looking at a blank screen, thinking it hadn't recorded, there it was. The first client—a smartly dressed guy, seemingly in his early fifties—arrived at about 2:30 in the afternoon. He requested that Paulene massage him. She had the main room upstairs in the front of the house. What would have been a bedroom was very nicely fitted as a massage room, with the massage table in the centre, a chair in the corner to put the clients' clothes on, a desk in the corner for making future appointments, and a sink on the wall with handwash and some shelves at the side of it with clean towels. It also had a fan for when it was too hot and a heater for when it was too cold.

The guy entered the room, and Paulene greeted him with a kiss on his cheek, which Sharon thought was rather warming. Then Paulene turned her back to him and asked him to unfasten her bra. She turned to him, revealing her naked breasts, and offered to help him undress. She undressed him slowly, folded his clothes very meticulously, and hung them over the chair. After that, she asked him to lie face down on the massage table. She poured some massage oil into her hands and gradually smothered him with it, being careful to cover every inch of his skin, including the crevice of his arse and his balls. As she was applying the oil, she leant down so that her tits could mischievously dangle all over his naked body. Then she started to massage him in a very sensual way. Nothing to do with the massaging Sharon had been doing, it was just very sensual and gentle.

THERE WAS A MUSIC CENTRE in the room. Paulene played a very relaxing CD so the client could hear the gentle music as she was swaying and gliding all up and down his body. After about half an hour, she climbed onto the massage table, put one leg on either side of him, and just let her tits and her vagina slide up and down his back and arse. This went on for about ten minutes. Then she got him to turn over, and she repeated the same action down the front of his body. By this time, he couldn't keep his hands to himself any longer, so he cradled her head with his hands and pulled her down towards him, and he fucked her vigorously. That was the beginning of the massage parlour's transformation.

THAT WAS THE DAY THE massage parlour became a brothel. Sharon wasn't sure whether it was the right thing. The girls were only meant to give massages with happy endings. But people were only human, and one thing led to another, and at the end of the day, who was it hurting? The men were chilling out and enjoying themselves. The girls were consenting adults and earning some decent money; they were sensible enough to know what happened in that room stayed in that room. And even if Sharon said they weren't allowed to have sex with the clients, they probably would anyway. So Sharon didn't say anything.

Sharon was fair to the girls. She didn't expect them to pay her half of what they earned; she only ever charged them £20 per client for the use of the facilities. Her attitude was *If they want to sell their bodies, it's their choice,* and she didn't want any part of it. If the girls charged £200, she still only took £20 per hour.

It wasn't long before other girls turned up wanting to work at Sharon's. Word was getting round. The first girl who turned up was a very pretty blonde girl from Russia. Her name was Anica. She was around 40 and very sexy. And another girl came from the Czech Republic, and one from Colombia. They just turned up ready to work. The more girls there were, the more clients came.

Once the place was established, the guys started phoning at ten o'clock in the morning, wanting to know which girls were on today. If it was a girl they liked, they would make an appointment. If the one they wanted wasn't on, they would phone back on the day she was on. The house was on the main road, so if a client was passing, knowing that there were sexy girls in the house, they couldn't resist the temptation of popping in to see the girls. So they would just turn up at the door.

The place became so busy Sharon actually had seven rooms as treatment rooms. She had the garage converted into a treatment room with a shower and toilet, and two rooms at the bottom of the garden, which used to be brick sheds, were rebuilt and turned into massage rooms. So in a day, there could be seven to ten girls on site, doing their own thing. Some would be making some food to eat, some would be doing their hair, some would be doing their nails, and some would be outside smoking cigarettes, not drugs. No drugs were ever allowed in the house. Suddenly, the doorbell would ring, and a guy would be there. He would come in and choose a girl. Then someone else would turn up, and within fifteen minutes, three or four girls would be working. It was always important to have plenty of girls in. You never knew how many men would turn up.

Because the house was in a busy part of London, there were men of many nationalities. There were Indian, Irish, West Indian, Jewish, Chinese, and many others. Over religious holidays, business would be quiet. Then, when the holidays were over, it would be busy again.

The girls were of many nationalities too. Some of the girls would sleep in the massage rooms when they came. One girl who turned up was from Lithuania. She was about eighteen, very pretty, with hair right down her back. She was called Cloe. She was married to a black man and had a baby with him. She also had a child in Lithuania, which her mother was caring for, so she needed to work to send money home. The clients thought she was lovely, and all wanted to see her. She was very busy. One guy fell in love with her, and eventually, after about two years, he left his wife and went to live with her. She left and wasn't seen again for about three years. Good thing there were plenty of other girls.

There was another girl from the Czech Republic; she used to come and go. She was in university and came back to pay her education bills and survive. She had a client, an old retired headmaster. He used to turn up with a briefcase and dressed in a suit. He always requested this girl Nicky. He liked her because she was small and looked like a little girl. Nicky said he had clothes in his briefcase. He would take out a gymslip, a blouse, white ankle socks, and a cane; tell her to put these things on; and play teacher and pupil with her. He would tell her she had been very naughty and bend her over his knee and cane her. The more she touched him and the more her bottom got red, the more excited he got. This was the only way he could get stimulation.

There was a very tall, slim blonde girl who also worked there. She was from Slovakia, but she didn't want anybody to know where she came from, so she said she was Swedish. She called herself Anica. She was a very beautiful girl. She had a young daughter, and she was living with her boyfriend, who also had a daughter. They had been living together for about four years. He knew where she worked, but he thought it was a beauty parlour, and he thought she was a nail technician. She worked at Sharon's for about two years.

One night, Sharon was massaging a guy in her flat on her own when a guy phoned up and asked if she did water sport. She innocently said, 'What is that?' He hung up the phone. So she asked her client she was massaging, 'What is water sport?' He didn't answer. She continued with the massage.

When the guy was finished, he showered and dressed and paid her, and just as he was leaving, he said to Sharon, 'Water sport is when a woman pees on a man's face.' With that information, he went off down the stairs and left Sharon surprised.

Later on, a demand for water sport did arise in Sharon's profession. There were certain guys who requested it. A girl would have to be experienced in doing it and want to do it. They would pay her good money for it. While the guy was lying face up on the massage table, she would have to get on the table, perch astride his face, let a few drops of wee go over his face, and then stop. She had to have good control to be able to stop and start it. She would do this for as long as she could manage it. This would get him very excited. Then they would decide between the two of them what took place after that.

All the girls worked to suit themselves. Most of the girls had their regular clients. The guys felt happy with a girl they knew and had a special rapport with. Most of these guys were in happy relationships and had children. Coming to Sharon's didn't interfere with their private lives. Every man was different and wanted different things. Some just wanted a little bit of sex in the afternoons; some craved what they could not get in their own homes.

There was a rather attractive guy who used to regularly see Anica. And one afternoon, Anica and he appeared in the kitchen, and Anica was a little worried. She told Sharon that her client was going to give her a lift to the pharmacy to get the morning-after pill because when they had been in the midst of fucking, all of a sudden, the condom had split. What she hadn't realised was when you use massage oil on a condom, the condom will disintegrate. She didn't want to get pregnant, so she left early to go to the pharmacy. Sharon and the other girls didn't see her for a couple of days.

When Anica did turn up, she looked very tired. Her eyes were very red, and she was crying. Sharon asked her what was wrong, and she said that the same day she had left work early, she and her boyfriend had made love at night, and he had found a piece of condom inside her. At that, all hell broke loose. He got his daughter out of bed in the middle of the night, put a few clothes in a black bag, got into his car with his daughter, and drove off into the night, never to be seen again. Anica was devastated. She left Sharon's after that and continued with her other work, in beauty. The clients missed her and kept asking if Sharon knew where she lived. Sharon thought that the attractive guy wanted to leave his partner for her, but he couldn't find her.

One of the customers, Michael, was a very tall man, about six feet four inches, and very broad, seemingly in his early fifties. When he came for a massage, he always asked for Sharon. He used to bring a ruler along. He would get the normal massage, and after about half an hour, he would get Sharon to use the ruler on his bum. So she would spank his bum as hard as she could over and over again until it was red and raw. The redder it got, the more he wanted it. He would wriggle around, and the more he wriggled, the more she spanked him. Sometimes, the ruler would break. Once he had had enough of the discipline, he would want to be a slave; he would beg Sharon to open her legs and allow him to reach up into her vagina and lick her profusely until she reached climax. Then she would have to wank him off to bring the performance to a close. Another satisfied customer. He bought lots of rulers.

Another girl who came to work at Sharon's was a white South African. She didn't say much about herself; nobody knew much about her. All they knew was that she was very busy, and every time she went into a room with a client, she would take in a fresh bowl of water. It appeared that she was giving them bed baths. It's every man's fancy when in hospital that a pretty young nurse would give them a bed bath. So this girl would dress up in a nurse's uniform and give all her clients a bed bath.

Men have to have regular sex, and they have to have variations. As someone once said, 'Even if you like steak, you don't want to have it every night. Sometimes, you need to go out for a hamburger.'

A lot of the old men would choose the Chinese girls. Although the girls were in their early thirties, they looked only about 14 because they were so small and boyish. Maybe the men fantasised they were with children to fulfil a forbidden fantasy. Sometimes, they would choose two girls and experience a double whammy.

Everybody had their different reasons for coming. Some older men had stopped having sex at home because their wives didn't want it anymore. Some were in arranged marriages and wanted to explore different activities. Some had wives who were ill, so they were just carers. Quite a lot of men had split up with their wives and didn't want to get into another relationship. They didn't want to introduce another woman to their children. Some men were just addicted to sex. Some men couldn't get into a relationship because they were disabled.

One guy came to the parlour because he was unfortunate to have had polio when he was a baby, and it left him with a twisted body. He lived in a home. The only time he was ever going to have any kind of intimacy was if he paid for it. So he regularly came for a massage and hand relief. It was probably the most exciting part of his day. He must have felt very relaxed after his treatment.

There was another disabled man who didn't have any hands. He had tried to commit suicide. He had gotten stuck on an electric power pole; they couldn't get him free, so they had to cut his arms off. When he came for a massage, Sharon had to do him. She would remove his coat and his shirt; then she would have to remove his prosthetic arms, which were taped to each other, so the tape would go round his neck and then connect to his stumps. Sharon was the only one who could do this. She would remove all his clothes and help him onto the massage table on his stomach, then start the massage. She stripped down to her knickers so he could enjoy the softness of her skin moving up and down his torso. Then she turned him over to find his hard, rather large penis, and it was eager for her to caress it, which she did eloquently. She teased him for a while, knowing that he couldn't interfere. He would rotate and wriggle until he couldn't take it anymore. Then she would have to do the deed. Once she cleaned him up, she would have to take him to the shower, wash him, and dry him. Then she put his arms back on and dressed him, got him all back together again, and sent him on his way, one very happy bunny.

The Chinese girls were very popular. They liked to work together. Men were always requesting a two-girl massage. The girls would strip off all their clothes. One girl would get straight on the guy's back and slide all the way up and down his back several times while the other girl would rub her hairy pussy all around his head and around his face. They would do this for about ten minutes; then they would turn him over, and one girl would slide her naked body down his face; she would slide her rather small breasts all around his face, and up and down his very hairy chest. While she was doing that, her pussy would be covering his wide-open mouth so he could absorb it all the way in. The other girl would climb onto the table and straddle the guy, and the girl stretched over the guy on the table would start licking the girl who just climbed onto the table. So both the girls would be getting licked at the same time.

When one guy had had enough licking pussy, he lifted the one girl gently to one side and pulled the other girl onto him so he could get his penis inside her and fuck the arse off her. She was more than ready; he clenched his hands around the cheeks of her bum and thrusted her body up and down with a vengeance while she groaned with delight. The more she groaned, the harder he penetrated. Her friend, who was watching, started playing with herself. Once the girl on the table had reached her climax, she let out a very loud scream. She got off the table so that her friend could stride the very large, firm, eager penis. Then it was her turn to get a good fucking. After about ten minutes, they both climaxed together, and the girl just collapsed on top of him. They rested. Then the three of them showered together. There was a shower in all the rooms.

They all dressed. The window was opened, the table was cleaned, and all the couch roll was disposed of. The room was sprayed, ready for the next customer. When they all came out of the room, no one but Sharon knew anything other than a massage had been going on.

Nowadays, men can last quite a lot longer when fucking because they will take Viagra, which can be bought on the internet. So they are well equipped when they come to a massage parlour. Once a man has had sex, he feels on top of the world. He pays the girls, then probably goes back to work and has a successful day and goes home to his family very relaxed.

There was a girl who came from the Philippines. She had been only 21 years old when she married a 62-year-old man named Terry. While he had been paying for her family to survive in the Philippines, she had been happy to stay married to him. After a couple of years, the money dried up, and she had to get a job. She didn't have any qualifications, so she wasn't able to earn much money. So she left her husband and asked if she could work for Sharon. Sharon had to put her up, but Sharon didn't mind that because that meant she always had a girl available if there wasn't anyone working.

Mary did do a very good massage. The Filipinos have a natural instinct for massage, so she was quite popular. The first weekend she worked, she earned £300. When Sharon gave it to Mary, she just hugged Sharon and cried. She had never seen £300. She sent every penny back to the Philippines for her family. She sent it by Western Union. Her mother would work all week, carrying boxes on her head all day for about £2 per week. So when Mary sent the money home every week, the family must have felt they had won the lottery.

Mary was a very hard-working girl. She worked at Sharon's for quite a long time; in fact, while Sharon was in prison, she lived in the house by herself and kept busy. Mary met a very nice guy, and it is understood that she married him and moved to America. Hopefully, she has her own family.

ANOTHER GUY COULDN'T MASTURBATE ON his own; he needed the help of a female. He turned up and said that he needed to wash his bum before having his massage, so he asked to use the bidet (a basin that is installed into European bathrooms). Sometimes, English people have bidets in their homes; it just so happened that there was one in this flat. So he removed all his clothes and strode over to the bidet facing the bathroom wall.

This bidet had a fountain-type tap that squirted water up into your bum. As he started getting quite wet, he asked Sharon if she would assist him by soaping his anus, which she did. This was turning him on, which inspired her to massage his very erect penis at the same time. He was squirming around on the bidet, getting more and more excited. He asked her to rub harder and harder and to grip as tightly as possible. Then, finally he came. That was okay because there wasn't any cleaning up—just let the tap wash it all away.

Sharon said, 'Would you like to get on the massage table and have your massage now?' but he said, 'No, I am fine now. I'll just get dressed and be on my way, if you don't mind.'

Sharon said, 'It's up to you.' She charged him £30, and he left. He felt relieved. That was all he wanted.

Sharon had learnt that everyone is different. All have their own special needs. Sharon worked hard every single day. Every day, a client would ask for something different.

One guy arrived very well dressed in a smart suit. He owned a news agent's in the centre of London. When he removed his clothes, he was wearing stockings and a suspender belt. He said, 'I would like to be massaged with them on, if you don't mind.' Well, each to his own.

Sharon gave him a very relaxing massage; it felt different to massage a guy's legs with nylons on. She massaged him for about forty minutes, and as she went to the top of the table, suddenly, his right hand went down from across his face to reach Sharon's left leg. His hand started wandering up and down her leg, from the ankle to the top of her thigh. Then he said to her, 'Next time I come for a massage, would it be okay if I bring you some nylons to wear?' and 'Would you put them on for me?' She agreed. That aroused him, so he took her hand and pressed it firmly onto his very erect penis.

Sharon was never bored to make contact with an erect penis. Every one of them was different. There were thin ones, fat ones, hairy ones, circumcised ones, very badly foreskinned ones, black ones, pink ones. Some had nodules; some were shaped like bananas. Some were so large she didn't have enough hands for them, and some were so very tiny. Over the years, Sharon observed that the men with very narrow shoulders and sunken stomachs had the largest penises.

Another of the regular clients at the massage parlour was a Polish man called Frederick. His parents had been killed in a concentration camp during the 1939–45 war. He had been evacuated to safely stay with a family in the north of England.

While growing up, he had been told that sex was both dirty and dangerous, in the sense that he could easily get a girl pregnant, and even if he didn't, as long as he had sex with her, she could say that he had to stay with her. So he had never had full penetrative sex with anyone and never married. He had never fallen in love and never trusted himself or any woman enough to have sexual relations. He must have spent all his life masturbating.

As he got older, he found it harder and harder to pleasure himself. So he used to go to a legitimate lady masseuse for the relaxation he needed. That kept him going for several years. Then one day, his masseuse told him she was retiring. She advised him that he should look in the paper for another massage service, and as long as the advert said *ITEC registered*, it would be legitimate, and he would get a proper massage. So he booked an appointment at Sharon's because it was ITEC registered. He came along, looking forward to getting a lovely massage.

The girl was very professional at first, and Frederick felt very relaxed. She massaged him for about forty-five minutes, and then she told him to turn over. Much to his pleasant surprise, when he turned over, she was topless. That got him very excited. She allowed him to touch her large, very firm breasts for a while. Then her hand went down to his genitals and started caressing them gently. His mind was blown with excitement, and he very quickly ejaculated. After that, he was so whenever he had some money to spare, he would make an ntment and have another massage. This went on for several years.

After a time, he needed a little more stimulation, as he wasn't getting any younger; he was well into his seventies. He asked if one girl could do the massage and another girl could come in and just do the end part if he paid her £10. That was agreed to as long as she was prepared to take her top off so that he would have four breasts to ogle at and touch. By that time, the guy was eighty-two and still going strong. They say a man is active until he dies; Sharon thought there was some truth in that.

When Frederick said that he still felt guilty coming to Sharon's, she asked him, 'Who really worries?' Absolutely nobody.

THERE WAS ANOTHER GIRL WHO came from South Africa and was extremely good looking, small, and dainty with cropped blonde hair. She was very slim and top heavy. She thrived on sex and really enjoyed her job. When the doorbell rang, she rushed to the door before any of the other girls got there. Then, when she opened it, she would say that all the other girls were busy and she was the only one available. She would be wearing a very tight top without straps, held up by her enormous breasts; tight white jeans that just came a little past her knees; and very high red heels with her toes poking through.

She would show the client into the downstairs room before the other girls saw him, undress him, and tease him while she was doing it. Then she would get him to undress her, and she would lie face down on the massage couch. She didn't believe in working after a few minutes. Then she would get him to use toys on her. Men wouldn't argue. It was all fun, and what man doesn't enjoy some fun?

She was an attractive girl, and the guys liked her. The other girls made life difficult for her, so it wasn't long before she decided to leave. But before she did, she planned to get her own flat and take her clients with her. So she became quite friendly with the electrician who worked for Sharon, and she got him to lend her £500 to help her get the money together to get the flat. She said once she moved in, she would start making regular payments, so he believed her and gave her the money.

She got the flat and set herself up, and she got Sharon's boyfriend to help her move. He came back smelling of whisky. And the mind boggles as to what went on that afternoon. Sharon's boyfriend's lips were sealed, and the electrician never got his money back.

A GUY PHONED SHARON'S PLACE TO ask if they could dress him up as a woman. They told him it was no problem; then he made an appointment for later that day.

He was a tall, thin guy with a soft voice. He said he'd been looking for this kind of service for quite a long time. They asked him how long he'd been dressing up. He said he'd been doing it all his life. He normally did it in secret. But now, he wanted to go public.

His name was Georgina when he was dressed up. After he finished his coffee, they went into the upstairs room near the bathroom. The first thing to do was his make-up. They used Sharon's because they didn't think the colour he'd brought along in a plastic bag was appropriate. The colour was too heavy. They had to clean and shave his face, use astringent to close the pores, put moisturiser and foundation on, and wait for it to dry. It's important to get the base right. Then they subtly added a little lip liner and a hint of green eye shadow to match his long, straight blond wig with a half fringe, which curved lightly over the side of his forehead.

He'd brought a white poplin blouse with a white lapel-type collar so it could stand up. It was matched by a black-and-white-checked suit with a long, sleek skirt with a split up the back. You could see right to the top of his legs. He had greyish-black stockings and suspenders, plus black three-inch heeled shoes with open fronts and a black shoulder bag. He did look rather good. Once he was ready, he wanted to sit down with the girls for a while, and they made him very welcome.

One of the regular clients said to him for a joke, 'Can I see her?'

He went red with embarrassment and said, 'Maybe some other time.'

After all that effort, he wanted to go out dressed as a woman. So he caught a bus and went to Brent Cross, that big shopping mall. He was out for quite a few hours. He came back exhausted. He said that it had been nerve-racking at first, but he did enjoy it and would definitely like to do it again. It was very discreet, with no harm to anyone. They charged him £30. He said it was the best £30 he'd ever spent. He changed back into his men's clothes and took off his make-up and went home very happy. He came back many times after that.

George could be Georgina whenever he felt the need.

Then came a couple of girls. Simon was from Ireland, and the other one, named Margaret, was from Scotland. They were both very tall with light brown hair and in their middle thirties. They came to work on Thursdays and Fridays. They were more the professional type and wanted to earn big money. They said they usually did the clubs in the West End, like Stringfellows, but they had heard about Sharon's place, so they thought they would give it a try. Sharon didn't know too much about professional prostitution, but she was prepared to give it a try.

When the clients knew there was someone new, they all wanted to see them. So these girls were quite busy for the first few weeks. They weren't too interested in doing massage, though. When they went into the room with the men, they would give them a menu and a price list. Most men chose the two girls—both girls completely naked, just wearing very high stilettos and a scarf round their necks. One would go to the head of the table and dangle her very large breasts gently over the man's face, and he would start to lick them as they swerved over him while the other girl would climb onto the table and gently slide her well-oiled body up and down his body. Then whatever they had agreed to at the beginning of the session, they would carry out. They would do anything as long as the guy was prepared to pay. This could be anal, two girls licking each other while he wanked himself off, or one girl fucking him while the other one had her pussy licked. Or just the two girls licking each other and maybe using a dildo on each other.

These girls had no barriers. They didn't stay long—only about four weeks. The men soon tired of them and stopped booking them. So they moved on, back to the West End probably. When the girls left, they did not mention that they wouldn't be back. They knew they were not coming back, so they didn't bother to pay Sharon. They were supposed to leave the money in the safe, but they didn't do so. That was the clue that they were not coming back. Sharon lost out every time. She charged only £20 for the use of the room. But those girls couldn't respect that.

Men are funny. The girls were a novelty at first, but men soon tired of them, or maybe their West End prices. Men want what they cannot have, and when they get it, they don't want it. Men are happy with a massage while they are being massaged; they don't know what is going to happen next. So they just enjoy the massage and anticipate what the girl has in store. A massage is always good for your well-being, physically and mentally. What happens after that is a bonus. Men don't like admitting that they are paying for sex. So by doing it in the form of a massage, they don't feel quite so guilty in this business.

There was a girl called Catherina, blonde, about five feet five inches tall, who was very busy. She always wore low-cut tops and very short skirts, sometimes with very loud, thigh-high, shiny patent-leather boots. She was with Sharon from the first week she opened, before the big influx of Polish girls.

A local guy, about fifty, called Michael started coming to see her. He lived on his own. Michael got very keen on Catherina and began seeing her twice a week, paying at least £100 each time. She would only see him when he was prepared to pay for a massage. After a while, he started giving her lifts home, and on the way, they would stop for a drink. This went on for several months. Then one day, she went into the massage parlour and said she had to go back to Russia for a while. And she left.

A couple of months went by, and one day, Michael phoned and asked if he could come along and have a chat with Sharon. She said, 'Yes, okay.' He turned up on a Friday, looking as though he had lost a lot of weight.

He said, 'Have you heard from Catherina?' He was clearly suffering from a broken heart.

She said, 'No. When they go, we don't know if they are coming back.' In this profession, nothing is for certain. The massage business is a very unstable life.

Catherina had told him she loved him and he was very special. The poor man was head over heels in love with her. She had said she needed money urgently and asked if he could get her a £20,000 loan, and when she came back, she would pay him back £500 per week from her work. He had believed her and gotten the loan, and he hadn't seen her since. He had borrowed the money from loan sharks, and they were after him. He was so scared of them that he gave up his flat and went to live with his brother in Brighton. The poor man was devastated. A truly broken man.

About a year went by, and Sharon received another phone call from him. He asked her if he could come along for a chat. So a couple of days later, he turned up, looking much better. He had put on the weight that he had lost. He said Catherina was in the car; she was too embarrassed to come in. He said they had gotten together and things were good between them now, and they were going to get married. He asked Sharon, 'Would she be able to get her job back?'

Sharon agreed to let her come back to work. At the end of the day, Catherina had had her problems, and they weren't anything to do with Sharon. She always seemed to be a pleasant person. The customers liked her, so why not let her back? So a few days later, she came back to work.

Michael and Catherina did get married, and her son came over from Russia to live with them, and everybody was happy. Catherina stayed with Michael for about five years, but the marriage did deteriorate. Michael started drinking again, and they constantly fell out. Catherina stayed at Sharon's right until the day the business closed down, when Sharon went to prison. At that time, Catherina got a job as a security lady and met someone else. Who knows what happened to poor Michael.

Another man named Alistair would call up every day and say, 'Anyone new?' His fetish was to be the first to see a new girl. His backside had to be the first one she touched. He took pleasure in explaining to her what she had to do because he liked to think that he could play teacher.

If Sharon told him that a girl was coming in at one o'clock for an interview, he would turn up at 12:30 so she could see him straight away. If Sharon said there was a new girl coming, he would sometimes come straight from the airport. He liked to pay £10 less, as he felt that he was a special friend. He once told a girl that he had to vet her for Sharon. He used to phone her every day, even when he was abroad in China, Australia, Brazil, or America, as he was always afraid that he might be missing something.

A smartly dressed middle-aged man called James would always

come around seven in the evening, after he finished work. He claimed that his work was for MI5 and very hush-hush. He would always sit and talk with the girls for an hour before choosing one or two. The first thing he would ask for was a glass of water so he could take his pill (a blue one).

He used to see a girl called Tracy, who also did a double act with another girl. They said he wore nylon stockings and suspenders and would enjoy the girls' doing a double act on each other. He would sit and wank himself off while he was eagerly watching them. After he reached his climax, the girls would give him a 'rainbow shower' (wee on him). He was so addicted to this he never missed a week. Every Thursday night, like clockwork, he would turn up. He had the money, so he paid the girls handsomely and went back to his chauffeur-driven car and home to his family.

THE FOLLOWING IS A CLIENT'S view on the need for brothels.

I'd been married for more years than I could remember. Through life's various highs and lows, I'd emerged safe but dissatisfied. There was something missing in my life. After a lot of thought, I recognised what it was. With time on my hands after retiring, I could now prowl the internet, looking for sex. A few clicks, and I came across Sharon's massage services. This seemed like the perfect solution for the gap in my life. I was in a relationship that no longer provided the physical comforts or the stimulation that I craved. The discovery of Sharon's services seemed likely to fulfil my needs discreetly.

I made an appointment and eagerly went along in anticipation of what I was getting into. I arrived there, pressed the bell, and was greeted by Sharon herself. She was very tall with long, very dark hair and had very large breasts that were struggling to stay inside her blouse. It was difficult to assess her age—younger than me, that was for sure—an attractive lady.

She showed me into a small massage room with a massage table in the centre of it. There was a trolley on the side wall with all the massage oils on it, and a chair for my clothes and a shelf with clean towels on it. The room was dimly lit, and there was relaxing music playing softly. As nervous as I was, I very soon started to feel relaxed as I was lying on the massage table. And I could feel the first drops of oil making contact with the skin on my back. Her hands were smooth and gentle but increasingly firm.

She moved round the table, focusing professionally over my body. She worked all over my body, first on the sides and top of my back and gently down my legs. Very soon, my eyes started to close in relaxation.

However, when her hands reached my buttocks and started massaging near my groin, I was no longer relaxed. My body stiffened in the most uncomfortable way. The expected excitement that I was hoping for was about to happen. She stood in front of me, and I managed to raise my head to look at her. I thought I had gone to heaven. Momentarily, I had a vision that she had taken off all her clothes, bar just a small pink pair of panties.

Her naked and voluptuous breasts were perfectly formed with dark, protruding nipples. With my head down on the table again, she leant over me and started to massage my neck and shoulders. Her breasts enveloped me as her hands gently and firmly moved down my back. What actually excited me was the musky aroma emanating from beneath her skimpy panties, behind which I could just make out some curly dark hair. She had become as excited and aroused as I was. I took a deep breath of that tantalising smell of sex that she was exuding. My head was floating. Sharon then moved to the side of the table and asked me to turn over. This relieved the pressure on my erection.

One day just before New Year's Eve, quite a few girls worked until eight o'clock, when most of them went home. There were just two girls working after that.

One girl named Annette had not had any work that night. At about 9:45, a guy rang and asked if he could come along at about 10:30. The house was fitted with CCTV cameras, and they could see who was at the front door. So Annette said yes, it was OK to come, although the house usually closed at ten o'clock.

At 10:30, the buzzer went. Annette looked at the camera and saw the guy standing there, so she opened the door to let him in. As she opened it, the guy pulled a very long knife on her, put it close to her neck, and pulled her long blonde hair, which was tied back. He said, 'Take me to the safe, bitch.' The poor woman was scared for her life.

As the guy pushed her back along the hall, two other men, also with long knives, came in with him. They had been hiding at the side of the house, out of view of the cameras. One followed them inside, and the other one went upstairs to see if there were any girls there. Annette showed one man to the safe, where he tried to get it open with a knife, and Annette was saying that the boss had been by and taken the money out, and he was on his way back to lock up. The second guy was emptying out the other girl's bag, looking for the money she had earned that day. He took it, and then he started hitting her around the head.

Then he went to Annette and emptied her bag and took some money that she had in it. She was screaming for them not to kill her; she said she had a young daughter. The second guy tried to get the television off the wall, and the third man came down from upstairs.

After the three guys had a good look round the downstairs, they opened the front door and ran off.

Annette then phoned Sharon; she was completely traumatised. Sharon came round within ten minutes. She wanted to call the police, but Annette wouldn't let her. She said she didn't want to go to court, and she didn't want her picture in the papers, so Sharon didn't phone the police.

It wasn't until a few days later that Sharon was able to get the CCTV tapes because she wasn't a technical person. When she did see the tapes, she was horrified, and she had to phone the police. They came round and checked for fingerprints and asked questions. They couldn't understand why it had taken a few days for Sharon to call them. That didn't go down too well. Ultimately, they were unable to get fingerprints because quite a few other people had been on the premises since the attempted robbery.

ANNETTE WAS SO TRAUMATISED SHE didn't come back to work again; neither did the other girl. It wasn't very long after that Sharon got arrested, as the police had decided to put surveillance on the house after the robbery. They watched it from January to May.

THEN THERE WERE THE GUYS who wanted dominatrices. They asked to be tied up and strapped with a whip. The woman had to be dressed in black leather, including black leather gloves, and very bright red lipstick, long black boots past her knees, and very long black hair running wild down her back and breasts.

When such a man came into the room, she had to tell him to strip naked and sit on a bench. She had a voice of authority; she really commanded him to strip. While she was waiting for him to strip, she waved the whip in his face and at his arse, telling him to hurry up. He said, 'Yes, miss,' in a very mild voice once he was naked.

She tied him up with leather straps to a ring in the wall. Once his hands were tied, she then bent down in front of him, revealing her large, voluptuous breasts. He had a sneaky look. Then she tied his feet to rings in the floor. Once he was tied up, she proceeded to run her whip along his arms, gently up and down, then down his chest two or three times, then around his balls. Then his cock started to twitch and to grow. It started moving from side to side. She whacked it with the whip and told it to behave; that made it go down in shame. Then she pressed her breasts to his face and rubbed his face with them. She gently pressed them into the side of his face. His cock came straight up again in anticipation. She made him turn over. She had to untie him for this and retie him up. Now, he had his back to her. She then proceeded to whip his bum.

As the whip came down, he slightly flinched. She repeated it again and again. Then his bum started to turn red. So she stroked it with a feather duster on a stick. His cock started to get hard again. She gently sprinkled it with warm water from a water pistol and gave it a gentle rub. Once again, she whipped his arse, and he started rotating it and quivering from side to side. Then she went away and left him tied up for about ten minutes. After he had calmed down, she untied him, got him to lie on a massage table on his back, and tied him up again. She got onto the table and slid up and down, smothering his face with her tits and pressing her thighs into his now very hard cock. He begged her to untie him. But she wouldn't.

After several minutes of this torture, she got off the table, removing her leggings and leather thong. Then she climbed back on top of him and gently but firmly inserted his cock into her very wet, warm fanny. He gasped with joy as she slid up and down on it. He very quickly came, as the anticipation to have any kind of control was too much. As he lay there, drained and fulfilled, she removed herself from his body and left him there to sleep it off. She got showered, ready for the next client.

One of the guys the girls called Naughty Tony. He used to turn up at all different times of the day. Depending on when he happened to be passing, he would choose a girl over the telephone so that when he turned up, she'd open the door for him, they'd go to the bathroom, and they'd never get to the massage room. All you would hear was water flowing, lots of splashing around, grunts, and groans. Then he was down the stairs and out the door, all within about ten minutes.

One guy turned up in a chauffeur-driven Bentley, wearing a very smart Savile Row suit. He picked one of the girls and carried a bag into the room. The girl later told Sharon what he had in his bag: a baby bottle, oversized nappies, a rattle, and a bib. He undressed, put on the nappy and a bib, and then asked her to fill the bottle up with milk and feed him. Basically, he wanted to be treated like a baby, which she did, even to the point of patting him on the back until he burped. During all this time, not once did he request any sexual services. All the time was spent playing at mummies and babies.

One day, there was an enquiry about doing a husband and wife together. They came along in the evening, mainly to check out the house—whether it was clean, hygienic, and discreet enough. They were a couple in their early forties from Poland, who had been married for fifteen years and needed something to enhance their sex lives. They were rather good looking and very pleasant.

They booked an appointment with Sharon. They asked that she massage the wife first, then the husband. The wife had a shower first and lay face down on the massage table. Sharon put a towel over her back; then she mixed up the massage oil, rubbing it into her hands, and started her usual routine while the husband sat in the chair and watched. He suddenly took off all his clothes. He took some of the oil in his hands and joined in with the massage while Sharon was at the head of the table, doing the upside-down effleurage. He did the same from his wife's toes up to her buttocks. Sharon was going down her body, and he was going up.

Soon, the wife started getting aroused and wriggling about. He then came to the side of the table and pushed his very hard dick into her mouth. Sharon wasn't sure what to do at that point. So she massaged the wife's head and gently pulled her hair. Her hair was very long, going right down to her bottom.

After a few minutes, the wife tired of it, and she lay face down again. Sharon continued massaging her back. Her husband then slid his mouth all the way from her feet to her bottom. She lifted her bum off the bed so that he could reach her fanny and perform oral sex on her from behind. Then after a few minutes, he got onto the massage table, rapidly pushed his very hard cock into her fanny, and fucked her very hard. Sharon was spanking his behind to make him go faster.

ANOTHER CLIENT WAS ACTUALLY A masseur. He would go to Sharon's to relax and recharge when he was worn out from giving massages. He would choose two Chinese girls because they were small and could walk on his back. He would let them walk all over him for an hour, and then in the second hour, after he had recuperated, he would pay. He was a very large chap. That's why he needed two girls.

Then there was the settee wanker who called himself Richard. At first, by the way a phone conversation with him went, Sharon thought he was a genuine client. He was very pally. He started saying what a good pair of legs she had and how she looked good in her tight skirt. She went along with the conversation, thinking that he was going to book an appointment for a massage. He didn't, and she thought no more of it.

Then she would get odd, random calls from him. If she was busy, she'd be rude to him. If she wasn't doing anything special, she would speak to him. He was a pleasant guy. He liked to phone and speak to the girls, but they soon realised what his game was. He wasn't going to come spend his money. He just wanted to speak to a woman. Their theory was he lived on his own, and when he felt randy, he'd take all his clothes off, sit on his settee with the phone in one hand and his cock in the other, and get off on the conversation. That didn't cost him more than a local phone call, unlike the 190 numbers costing £1.50 per minute. This went on for eight years.

One day, having never met Richard, the girls told Richard, 'It's time you came and introduced yourself.' He did turn up later that day. He was quite a pleasant-looking guy, medium build, in his early thirties. They had a chat, and he left.

Then you've got the bored guys stuck on the motorway in delayed traffic, sitting there fed up to the teeth, thinking, *Who can I phone? All my friends will be working now. So why not phone a massage girl?* They always have time for a friendly chat. Sometimes, Sharon would be cooking dinner and have to time everything to cook together or fry meat for spaghetti bolognese, and the phone would ring. And it would turn out to be a time waster with nothing better to do.

Then there was a city gent in his pinstriped suit who was totally in love with himself. His specialty was choosing the most dominant-looking woman, possibly one in her fifties, and getting her to kick him in the testicles with pointed shoes or boots. The more pain he felt, the more excited he got. When he reached the peak, he would come like a volcano.

IN THIS BUSINESS, YOU GET all kinds of clients of all shapes and sizes. Some are easy to get on with, and some are difficult. Some are very clean, and some come in smelly and have filthy feet. Some are very chatty; some don't say a word. Some want everything for nothing; some tip well.

Sharon's place was like a home away from home. She was in her house for about twelve years before the police raided it, and most of the clients who were there when it shut down had been there from the beginning.

After several years of being on her own, Sharon met a man while at a dinner party at her sister's. His name was Tony. Tony was age 57 about six feet tall, slightly bald with dark hair, and he wore glasses. He was a rather good-looking guy. He worked for a taxi firm, doing executive driving. He mainly drove footballers and television stars around.

For a joke, Sharon invited him back to her place and pretended there was a party going on. So he accepted and followed her back. When they got there, she showed him into her lounge and then went into the kitchen to make a pot of tea. By then, it was around midnight. They talked and talked until about three in the morning.

Tony was very inquisitive and wanted to know everything about her life. He told her before he was a taxi driver, he was in the insurance business, until his business partner robbed him and he went bankrupt. So he was a knowledgeable man.

When it was time to go home, Sharon said, 'It's late, and you're tired. You can stay the night, but I only have one bed, and I snore.'

He said, 'That's OK, because I snore as well.'

So with that, Sharon had a shower and asked herself if she was doing the right thing, sleeping with a stranger and actually going to sleep. Having sex in the massage room was one thing. But this was different; this was letting someone into her personal life. It felt quite worrying, but it was too late now. She had already told him he was welcome to stay.

She got dried and slipped into bed. He used the bathroom; then he got into bed. It was quite nerve-racking. They had a peck on the cheek, and Tony said he had to leave at 6 a.m., as he had an early job.

So he turned around and went to sleep. Sharon couldn't get to sleep. She was afraid to relax. She did finally go to sleep, but it seemed to take a rather long time.

As 6 a.m. came round, she seemed to be in a deep sleep and didn't want to wake up.

TONY WAS UP AND ABOUT and ready to leave as she woke up. He kissed her gently on the cheek and said he would give her a ring and then left.

Later on that day, the phone rang, and it was Tony. He said, 'I know this is presumptuous, but can I come round tonight? I want to see you again. I will bring a takeaway.'

Sharon said, 'OK, but there is no need to bring a takeaway. I will cook some fish.' So he turned up at seven o'clock with a bunch of flowers. Sharon was impressed; she hadn't had flowers in many years.

They had the meal and sat talking for hours. It seemed that they had a lot in common. They got on like a house on fire. Sharon asked Tony where he lived. He said he was staying with an elderly aunt. Sharon believed him.

He stayed the night. They kissed and cuddled. But nothing else happened because Tony couldn't get it up. Sharon said, 'Not to worry; these things take time in the real world, not the massage world. People have to get to know one another. Everyone is different.'

The next day, Tony woke up early, went off to his job at 6 a.m., and said he would phone later. Sharon didn't see Tony for a couple of weeks. He kept phoning but had different excuses why he couldn't come round. Sharon didn't worry about it. She just got on with her business.

Then he turned up unexpectedly and said he'd been busy with his work. He also mentioned that he was going to Canada the following week to see his mother and sister. Sharon was envious of his going to Canada. So she said, 'I wish I was coming with you.'

He replied, 'You are welcome to come, but I'm afraid I cannot afford to pay your airfare. If you can pay that, I have a motel booked. You can come, Sharon.'

Sharon thought about it for a moment and agreed to go. She was more than happy to pay her own fare. So Tony booked a ticket for her. They were going on a Saturday.

Sharon got herself ready, and Tony came to pick her up at around 10 a.m. When he saw her at the door, he was pleasantly surprised by how nice she looked. Her make-up was very nicely done; she was wearing lipstick. Tony said, 'I have never seen you with lipstick on before. It is really nice. You look great.' That made

SHARON FEEL GOOD. TONY PICKED up the bags and placed them in the car. Off they went, both feeling very happy.

The plane journey was interesting because they had plenty to talk about. They had a couple of glasses of wine and got quite cosy together. They had a blanket over them, so they were able to kiss each other and play beneath the blanket. All in all, it was a very good flight.

When they arrived in Montreal, Tony's mother, Helen, and sister, Patricia, were there to greet them. Tony's mother asked Sharon if she was going to be her daughter-in-law, to which Sharon said, 'It's early days, but it could be possible.' They then all went back to Helen's for tea and bagels.

In the evening, Sharon and Tony went on their way to the motel. It was so cold in Canada that there was snow on the ground. Everywhere looked so white. When they arrived at the motel, it was so picturesque. They got out of the car and had to go up about eight steps to get to the room. Tony then opened the door, and the room was so large. It had two double beds in it, and it was lovely and warm.

Tony and Sharon unpacked, had a shower, and got into bed together and cuddled up. That was when they fell in love. It was a romantic start to the nice time they had with his family for three or four days.

One morning, Tony showed Sharon the subway. In Montreal, the subway has shopping malls in it, and cafes. As they were sitting in this little cafe that had red-and white-checked tablecloths, Tony reached across the table, took Sharon's hand in his, and asked her to marry him. So instantly, she said yes. They were both so happy; it was pouring down with rain when they came out of the subway, and they didn't even notice it.

The next day was Tony's sister's birthday and the day before Sharon's. So Tony arranged for them; Patricia and her two grown-up children, Mark and Lisa; and Helen of course to have dinner in a very smart restaurant. While they were enjoying the meal, Tony stood up and said, 'I have an announcement to make. Sharon and I are engaged.' He told them they didn't have a ring but that didn't matter. He said he would get very special wedding rings made instead; Sharon was OK with that.

SHARON AND TONY HAD BOTH been married before—been there, done that. The most important thing was to be happy. The wedding was to be on 15 April, only one month away.

They had a lovely week with the family, said their goodbyes, and went back to England. When they arrived home, Tony went to live with Sharon. The next day, he said he was going to his aunt's to get most of his clothes. When he arrived back, he looked quite sad. Sharon asked him, 'What's wrong?' but he wouldn't say.

Later on that day, the phone rang, and he went into the other room, so Sharon didn't know what he was talking about. This happened quite often. But Sharon didn't like to be nosy, so she never asked.

Then one day, she did ask. He replied that it was an old girlfriend he used to live with, and she was an alcoholic and was pestering him. Sharon accepted that, and they carried on with their plans.

When 15 April arrived, Sharon and Tony did get married. None of Tony's family members were there; his sons wouldn't talk to him after his breakup with their mother. Tony did invite a few friends from the Freemasons, which he was a member of. Sharon had her brother's sister and children—now adults—and her grandchildren there. Her parents had sadly passed away. The wedding was in a registry office, and there was a small reception at the Hilton Hotel in Bushey. The day went off very nicely. When they got home, Tony fell asleep, and that was the start of their new life together.

The next day, the phone rang. Tony had already left for work, so Sharon answered it and heard a soft female voice on the other end. She said, 'I am Mrs. Lunnon, and I want Tony to come home. He's my husband, and I miss him, and I can't live without him. He must come home.'

SHARON SAID, 'NO, YOU'VE GOT it wrong. I am Mrs. Lunnon, and he is married to me.'

She said, 'That cannot be. He is my Tony, and I want him to come home.' She told Sharon that he had been living with her for several years, and he had told her he was going to Canada to visit his mother and sister and then he would be back. She said she didn't know what happened to him, but he must come home. She couldn't live without him.

Sharon said, 'He is married to me now. We just got married.' The woman said she didn't believe it, so Sharon had to give her the address and the name of the registry office so she could get in touch with them and find out if this was true. She must have done her checks because Sharon never heard from her again.

Tony would never admit that he was still living with her at that time, but Sharon believed the woman. It made sense why she hadn't seen him in the beginning of their very short relationship before they went to Canada. If Sharon had known that, she wouldn't have entertained him. Still, what was done was done. She was married to him now, and whatever reason he had for his behaviour, only he knew.

As time went by, Tony was still working for the car-hire company, but was quite bored with it. He left home at 6 a.m. and didn't arrive home until 7 p.m., and after paying his expenses, he wasn't bringing very much more home. So Sharon suggested that she open another massage parlour near the tube station and he could run that. He would make more money than he was getting being out thirteen hours a day. As their relationship was going very well, Sharon didn't have any fears that he would step out of line.

HE REALLY WAS THE LOVING husband. Every Friday night, when he came home from work, he would come in with a big bunch of flowers. Weekends when he was home, he would always help with the cleaning, and he loved to cook. He was romantic and kind. The only problem was he needed Viagra for his erectile dysfunction. He had spoken to his doctor, and he had prescribed about four a month. So everything was happy.

After Sharon and Tony had a long chat about opening another massage parlour for him, they agreed to go ahead with it. The agreement was that Sharon would rent a flat above the shops in the town near the tube station. She would pay three months' rent in advance, have the flat in her name, and furnish it with three massage tables, covers, towels, massage oil, paper rolls for the tables, television, CCTV cameras, radio in the rooms, a walkaround phone, chairs, and equipment for the kitchen. She put an advert in the paper for more ladies to work at Tony's place. She said she would let some of her ladies work there until Tony got his own staff. When he got on his feet, he could start paying her back. It was all agreed.

Sharon found a two-bedroom flat, and Tony gave his notice to his work. And a few weeks later, the new massage parlour was opened. Tony was to be in complete control of this parlour. He was to pay the bills and run it. Sharon didn't want to be involved with it. When Sharon told the clients about it, they were happy because they could have a choice of two places.

Tony's place got quite busy fast. Soon, he got some new ladies, so the clients wanted to see the new ladies. Some days, he was busier than Sharon. Sharon didn't mind because she was still always busy. There was enough business for both of them.

When Tony got up in the morning, he would help Sharon with the cleaning. Then at about 10 a.m., he would go to his place to get it open and ready for the day. He was earning much more money now, so he was happy.

One day, a guy came in and offered Tony some Viagra for £2 a tablet. Tony thought he couldn't refuse this. He got only four a month from the doctor, so he bought an amount worth £50 and put the Viagra in the bedside cabinet.

For a while, everything was going well. Then one of Sharon's girls who had been working in Tony's flat said she had seen Tony come out of a room naked and head for the shower, and a massage girl was naked in the room. Well, Sharon couldn't believe what she was hearing. Tony was such a romantic husband. He would never do that.

So that night, Sharon asked him if he had enjoyed his massage. He nearly hit the roof. He said, 'How dare you accuse me of having a massage! That is very insulting.' He made such a big fuss out of it, Sharon decided she would never confront him again. She would have to find another way.

Tony's place had been running for a couple of years when one morning, Sharon was sitting in her kitchen, and she had a phone call from a guy saying, 'Is your other place open today? I have been ringing and ringing, and there is no reply.'

Sharon said, 'I don't understand that. Tony is there. He left to go there an hour ago.'

Bearing in mind Tony's place was only fifteen minutes away, Sharon wanted to go there and have a look at what was going on. But she knew if she went there, the girls would see her on the CCTV camera, and they would make everything look normal, so that would be a waste of time.

Eventually, Sharon found out a couple of girls from Russia in their early twenties, named Alger and Rosia, were at Tony's place in the evening after they closed up. A couple of businessmen who were regular clients would go there and bring them hot food, and they would eat and drink until the early hours of the morning. This became a regular occurrence. Then the guys invited the girls to go away with them for the weekend. And this really upset Tony.

Sharon asked him, 'What are you getting upset about? It's up to them what they do when they are not working. You have other girls.' It turned out that he was jealous.

THEN SHARON NOTICED THAT HIS supply of Viagra was diminishing rather quickly. Tony wasn't using the pills with her, so it was time to find out when he was using them. She tried talking to one of the girls. She said she didn't know anything.

It was said that when a new girl turned up for a job, Tony would make her massage him so that he knew whether she was good enough for the job. He would strip off naked on the massage couch, tell the girl to strip naked, and get her to give him a very sensual massage. Then he would have her do a *body-to-body*, which meant to get on the massage table and slide her body from his legs to his head, up and down. Then she would get him to turn over so that he was facing her and slide up and down, allowing her tits to slide on his face, down his hairy chest, down along his cock, over his thighs, and back up again. Then she had to wank him off. If it was satisfactory, she got the job. What an interview.

Tony was always getting new girls. He had some very attractive ladies. Tony seemed to be spending more and more time at the flat.

Tony was getting the girls to massage him every day. It was becoming an addiction, just like an addiction to gambling or alcohol. It was serious. At first, Sharon didn't realise it was getting to that point—that he was rushing the cleaning at her house so he could hurry up and get to the flat. But then, Sharon noticed that he was buying more and more Viagra. It seemed that the more massages he had, the more he wanted.

Then he started complaining that he didn't have any money—that the business was quiet. Sharon couldn't understand that. So she offered him a couple of her ladies to go work there to help him out. They didn't say anything at first. After a few weeks went by, they told Sharon that he was paying the girls to massage him as if he were a customer.

It seemed that the girls were only interested in earning money. That's why they did this job. Tony was an ageing man, in his early sixties, so to get them to do as he wished, he paid them as if he were a customer. That way, he could get what he wanted when he wanted. It got so bad that he couldn't pay the rent. He had become massage-and sex-crazy.

Eventually, one day, the girls who Sharon had sent to the flat told Sharon exactly what was going on. Sharon was devastated in her naïve way that she had trusted Tony and never thought it would come to this.

When Tony arrived at home that night, Sharon couldn't bring herself to talk to him. She was devastated and speechless. Tony was worried because he didn't know what was wrong with her. He kept saying, 'Why don't you speak to me?'

Then Sharon opened up and said, 'I know what's been going on. Get out. Take your clothes, and just get out. And I don't want to ever see you again.'

So Tony chucked his house keys on the bed and said, 'OK, I'll go.' He wouldn't take his clothes. He wouldn't take a thing.

Sharon said, 'Take your clothes.'

He said, 'Where I'm going, I don't need them.'

Sharon was frozen with disappointment. She had trusted Tony. They had started out being in love, and Tony had always been caring, kind, and thoughtful. When she had suspected something might be going on, she had dismissed it. She would feel guilty for ever suggesting that Tony would get involved with women who were servicing other men. She had thought he had more dignity than that. It wasn't as though they had no sex life together. At that time, she didn't know the depth of what an addiction could do. All she could think was that he had betrayed her and she was hurt.

Later on that night, she got a phone call from the Barnet police. They told her that Tony was in Barnet Hospital. He had taken an amount of paracetamol and a bottle of whisky, and they gave Sharon a patient number and told her what ward he was in if she wanted to come see him. Sharon didn't go to the hospital. She didn't want Tony to think that she forgave him. She didn't feel sorry for him; she was deeply hurt and certainly didn't want to see him.

The next day, not knowing if he was dead or alive, she went to their weekend home in Essex and stayed there for a couple of days.

Two days passed, and Tony rang her and asked if he could stay at their house. She told him he could stay if he wanted, but she wouldn't be there. So he got himself lodgings, and Sharon did not see him for a couple of weeks. Then, after she had calmed down, she helped him get a flat just along the road from her. She helped him furnish it, got some curtains, and fixed it up for him.

TONY LOST INTEREST IN HIS massage parlour after that, so Sharon had to run it. He went into a depression, and a few months later, he hanged himself. Poor Sharon, she felt responsible for this. She kept saying if she hadn't set him up with a massage parlour, it would never have come to this. She felt guilty for a long, long time. Sharon wore only black for about a year. She didn't go out—just kept running her business.

The neighbours wanted her to close down! Tony's place got closed down. The landlord came in, confiscated all the equipment, and changed the locks.

Now, Sharon was having trouble in her place. She was getting poison-pen letters saying, 'If you don't close down, you are going to be reported to the council and the inland revenue.' Sharon thought that was someone bluffing.

One day, the inland revenue turned up and searched the place, took any paperwork they could find, and left. Then a few days later, they phoned and made an appointment to come see Sharon. They asked how much equity was in her holiday home, and she said, '£120,000.' They said they would have that.

Sharon was a taxpayer and thought they were taking liberties due to the type of business she was in. So she got her accountant to deal with them. After a year of going through all the transactions, they agreed to £60,000, which Sharon had to pay.

About six months after that, on a sunny morning in April, Sharon had just had a meeting with a builder about getting some work done on the house. There were about six to seven girls sitting in her kitchen and dining room, with no clients that morning. Sharon had gone upstairs to use the bathroom. She was sitting on the toilet when she heard a rumpus downstairs. She thought it must be someone fighting, so she quickly pulled up her jeans and opened the bathroom door to have a listen. To her shock, there were plain-clothed male and female police officers on every stair with their backs to the wall, and one in front of the bathroom door, who said, 'Sharon Lunnon, I am arresting you for conspiracy to control prostitution.'

Sharon couldn't believe her ears. She thought they had made a mistake. She thought that after she spoke to them, they would go away. She said, 'Just a minute. I am on the toilet.'

The female officer let her go back in the bathroom, but she said, 'Hurry up.'

When Sharon came out of the bathroom, the officers wouldn't let her go back downstairs. They led her into the back massage room. Her phone was ringing, so they made her turn it off and leave it on the massage couch.

While Sharon was forced to sit on the massage couch, all the other police started searching the house. As they finished one room, they took Sharon into the next room. Meanwhile, police were downstairs questioning the girls. Sharon didn't know what was happening down there.

A couple of hours later, while the police were in the smallest room, which was used for an office, and Sharon was standing there, she said she needed to use the bathroom. So she used the bathroom, and when she came out, she saw her phone on the massage table and nobody guarding it. She grabbed it and put it in the pocket of her jeans. She was kept upstairs for about eight hours while the police went through every cupboard, drawer, bin, et cetera. They put everything in plastic bags, including the computers and CCTV cameras.

At about 8:30, it was time to go to the police station. Sharon said she needed to go to the loo before they went. While she was in the toilet, she put her phone in the bottom of the toilet brush holder.

When the police were ready to leave, they remembered they didn't have Sharon's phone. Sharon said she didn't know what had happened to it, so they decided to ring it. But they had told Sharon to switch it off, so that didn't work. So they started searching for it. They pulled out the bath panel, checked behind the radiator. But they did not find it. Ha ha.

Sharon was pushed into a car and driven to the Charing Cross Police Station, the main police station in London. Her handbag, bra, and belt were taken from her. She was searched and told to sit down and wait. The police officer behind the desk told her she was being charged with conspiracy to control prostitution.

Sharon waited for about an hour; then a police officer called her to have her fingerprints taken. There was a big problem with that because the fingerprints wouldn't come out. The officer must have tried four to five times. Then Sharon was told to wash her hands. That didn't work either, reason being Sharon had worn away her fingerprints from years of massaging. Then the officer also took a swab from her mouth.

It was about twelve or one in the morning when she was put in a cell for the night. She received one thin blanket and a sandwich (she was starving) and a paper cup of tea. There was a toilet in the cell with no seat and a bench round the walls. Sharon lay on the bench and tried to get some sleep. She was woken at about 6 a.m. by all the noise going on surrounding her. Sharon just lay there for hours; she didn't know the time.

Sometime during the morning, she was given some breakfast of an egg sandwich and a paper cup of tea. It must have been in the early afternoon when she was introduced to the prison solicitor, who told her that the police were going to interview her, but she didn't have to say anything; she should just say, 'No comment.'

So the interview got started. There was a female officer and a male officer. They warned her that it was being recorded. The interview got started, and Sharon said, 'No comment.' Then she got fed up with that and wanted to set the record straight, so she told the solicitor that she wanted to answer the questions because she didn't have anything to hide. So the solicitor agreed.

The interview went on for a couple of hours. At about eight o'clock in the evening, the police told her she could leave, but she would be on bail. She phoned her cousin to pick her up, and she went back to her house.

Due to the fact that she had been arrested, she didn't know whether she was allowed to carry on trading, so she phoned her solicitor and asked him. He said, 'They haven't shut you down, and if you say nothing untoward is going on, then it's up to you what you decide to do.' She decided to carry on but be a little more discreet.

About eighteen months later, the date of the court hearing came up. It was in May. The trial went on for three weeks. Sharon was worried that she would probably go to prison, but in her mind, she didn't think she deserved to go to prison because she let the girls live in her house. They treated it as if it were their own home. They were happy. They only worked the hours that they wanted to, and she only charged them £20 per hour for the use of the room, electricity, hot water, oils, towels, and couch sheets.

SHARON THOUGHT SHE WAS REALLY fair, so she hoped she would just get a fine and maybe some community service. So stood in the witness box and answered all the questions, and she told the judge she didn't take money for sexual services. What arrangements the girls made with the clients were their own business. They were private arrangements, she said. The £20 she charged the girls was for the use of the establishment—room and supplies.

The judge said, 'It doesn't work like that.' He said the girls paid £20 out of their earnings, so that amount was part of the sexual activities, and that made her guilty. In hindsight, if Sharon had charged the guys £20 to come in the door as an entrance fee, as the other massage parlours did, that would have been OK. So on 6 August 2007, Sharon got a fifteen-month sentence.

She started it at Holloway in London. Holloway is a famous prison in North London. It is famous because Ruth Ellis was executed there. When Sharon arrived, she had to stay in a dormitory with five beds and a little fourteen-inch TV that was always on religious programmes. The women in there were all different nationalities, mainly black women. There was one Filipino girl. They had plastic knives and forks and plates, and a black bin liner at the door full of rubbish. They stayed in that room all day, just went out for fifteen minutes in the afternoon for fresh air.

Sharon cried a lot for the first week. She really didn't think she should have been sent to prison. It wasn't as though she was trafficking women or giving them drugs or keeping their passports. She felt that she treated the girls really well. They made their choice, and they were all consenting adults. Nobody wanted them to do anything they didn't want to do.

THE SHOWERS WERE JUST DOWN the hallway and were quite decent. It looked like they had just been refurbished. There was plenty of hot water. The women were only allowed to shower in the morning.

At weekends, they were locked up most of the day. Sharon had been there only two days when on Friday morning, at 6:30, the warden knocked on the door and said, 'Mrs Lummon, get dressed. You're going to the police station now.' She was very worried, wondering what they wanted her to go to the police station for. All sort of horrible thoughts were going through her mind.

She went to the prison office to confirm that she had to go. They said yes, she did. They said, 'You have to take all your things with you.'

For one moment, Sharon thought she might have been bailed out. She hoped this might be the case because she was missing her dog, Bella.

Sharon wasn't allowed to take a shower. That upset her. She never went out without showering; she felt like a tramp. She was handcuffed to get into the *sweat wagon*, as they call it. And when she was inside, it was divided into separate compartments so the passengers could not touch one another. There were several other girls in the wagon, probably going to different prisons or other courts. They all had to be strip-searched. The other girls were all quite noisy.

They arrived at Southwark Crown Court by nine o'clock. Sharon asked for a cup of tea, which took ages to arrive. She was starting to get a headache. She sat in the empty cell for about an hour with nothing to do or look at—not a magazine, nothing. While she was sitting there, a young girl came in wearing a grey tracksuit with a hood. Sharon asked her why she was there. She answered she had held a man down while someone threw acid in his face. Once Sharon heard that, she didn't want to speak to that person again.

Sharon sat there quietly until 11:45, when a policewoman came in and told her she had to go to a room. Sharon was very anxious because she still didn't know why she had been taken there.

When Sharon arrived in the room, she met a barrister. She had never met him before. He informed her that the meeting was just an administrative matter to tell her that the court costs were going to be collected together with the confiscation settlement. For that information, Sharon had had to endure all that anxiety. She was annoyed and disappointed at the same time. All she could do was burst into tears. She did go into the court for ten minutes, and the judge did apologise for calling her there that day. But the prosecution thought it only right that Sharon was there. What a sadist.

Sharon told her solicitor about it. She said they were treating her like a hardened criminal. She felt it was wrong because she knew she hadn't hurt anybody.

She managed to get some lunch at about 1:30. This was her first food of the day. She'd been up since 6:30 a.m. It was cruel, and she had a headache. After that, she had to sit in an empty room again until 3:15. Then they took her back to Holloway. The women in her room were pleased to see her back, and she was allowed a shower. She was exhausted and hoped that she wouldn't get any more days like that.

The next morning, while the girls were milling around in the cell, a girl came into the room for a chat and mentioned that she had a single cell. Sharon was interested to know how she was able to have her own cell, and she answered that she had banged her neighbour over the head with a hammer. That was how she had her own cell. Oh well, it was Holloway.

When the girls were allowed out for some fresh air, they chatted with the other inmates. Sharon got to talking to a 68-year-old Essex woman called Mum. She was in for armed robbery, for which she got twelve years. It was a big, well-organised crime. They had attempted to rob a stately home that stood in its own grounds. The house was supposed to have had a very large safe, so they had come armed with a few guns to blow it up. She said they had put a ladder up at one of the windows, and she had fallen off it. And as she had tried to get up, she had found herself surrounded by police.

THERE WAS ANOTHER GIRL CALLED Jan who had been in Holloway for six years and was hoping to be released next year. She was also in for armed robbery. Having been involved with a gang in the East End of London, Jan was now rehabilitated, and her job was to show people round the prison when they first came in. She was very thorough and made others feel as at home as possible.

The Saturday routine here was wake up at about 9 a.m., have toast and tea, shower, iron your clothes, and clean your room with your roommates. When that's done, lie on your bed, and read until lunchtime. Then have lunch. Then get locked in the room until three o'clock. Then the women were let out in the gardens for ten minutes for some fresh air and a chat with the other women. Then they were locked up again for the rest of the day to read or watch television or pray or do some writing.

Sharon just lay on her bed and thought about her family, so sorry for her son and daughter and grandchildren. She felt that she had embarrassed her children because her case was in all the newspapers and her daughter had a very responsible business. She had shamed the family. She kept beating herself up over it. The next day being Sunday, she was looking forward to her first visit from her daughter and son-in-law.

When she saw them, she hugged her daughter and cried a little and said to her daughter how sorry she was to bring disgrace to the family. Her daughter hugged her back and said, 'It's OK. Don't worry about it.'

Then they sat down, and her son-in-law went to the hatch, where a lady was selling teas and coffees and biscuits. They all had a cup of tea and chatted for about an hour. When it was time to go, they had a quick hug and left.

SHARON FELT A LOT HAPPIER now that she had seen her daughter. Sunday was a good day.

After her family left, the women were allowed to sit out in the gardens for half an hour. Sharon was talking to a girl named Rose who was upstairs on the high-risk landing. She was in for ABH; she told Sharon that she had tried to kill her boyfriend. There was an Indian lady who was there because she killed her baby, put drugs inside the baby, and took it on an aeroplane. The air crew got suspicious when they noticed that the baby never cried.

After that breath of fresh air, Sharon went back to her room and watched television for the rest of the evening.

Monday was a busy day, with education at nine o'clock. Sharon went on a computer course.

In the afternoon, she went to meditation. When that had finished, they were allowed out in the gardens for their daily fresh air. Sharon was talking to a lady in a sari, not the kind of lady you'd expect to see in prison. Sharon asked her what she was in there for, and she said, 'Passport fraud.'

They had dinner and went to an evening class to learn word processing. Sharon had to do touch typing. She got up to thirteen words a minute.

Monday was a very busy day. Sharon was pleased to go to bed. When they were in their room, they were continuously getting locked in. They couldn't make sense of it. Then they realised that the riff-raff on the landing were fighting, so they had to be locked up for their own safety. It is very rough in Holloway. *These people are real criminals. The system is wrong,* Sharon thought. Sharon had a quiet life and didn't need to be with violent people like them.

The next day being Tuesday, Sharon's clothes arrived. So she was able to wear her own clothes. That made her feel better.

On Wednesday, 13 August 2008, Sharon was woken up at 7 a.m. and told she was moving to Morton Hall. So Sharon quickly got up and packed all her things into a dustbin bag and waited for instructions.

The next step was to be searched. Then they sent her to another caged wagon, and she received a packed lunch consisting of a sandwich, a chocolate biscuit, some crisps, and a plastic bottle of water. Then she and the other girls were driven down the A1 and onto the M1 motorway. The whole journey took about three and a half hours from door to door. There were six girls travelling, but they weren't able to speak to each other. There were two girls from Bulgaria who didn't speak English. They were crying because they didn't want to move far away from London; they had small children and thought they wouldn't make the journey so far away. It was sad.

Sharon felt apprehensive, thinking about what to expect on the journey. Everything had been such an ordeal. She was just settling in at Holloway. Now, it was all another upheaval: start all over again.

As prisons went, Morton Hall had very nice surroundings. It was out in the country, with lots of trees and pretty bushes and flowers, far away from the pollution of the traffic. It looked a bit like a health farm. There were about thirty ducks waddling around the grounds, regularly giving birth to broods of ducklings.

The place was once an RAF barracks. So it was set out with huts, which had been built in brick into prison quarters. It had its own farm, gym, library, education centre, health centre, and industrial area, where the women could work and earn their wages. They were all set out in the different corners. To get to all the different places, they did have to go outside and get written permission before they went anywhere. It was pretty cold there in the winter, especially when the girls had to queue up for their food.

BEFORE MORTON HALL WAS A women's prison, it had been a borstal. Then it had changed to a men's prison. It had only been a women's prison for five years. After Sharon left, it was supposed to be changed again, this time to a young offenders' institution.

Some of the prison officers were very pleasant, and some were bullies. There were a few Sharon really liked. They treated her as an adult. They were the sensible ones.

The food wasn't too bad. The prisoners were given a menu a week before so they could order their food for the following week, and they had plenty of fresh fruit every day.

Work was compulsory in Morton Hall, and there were a list of jobs available. Sharon chose machining T-shirts in the workshop. After she'd been in the factory for a while, they changed from making T-shirts to sewing jackets for the canteen staff. Wendy, the manageress of the factory, asked Sharon to cut out a pattern for the jackets. That was interesting because Sharon had been to dressmaking classes about thirty years before and had been shown how to cut a pattern. And then, of course, her grandfather had been a pattern designer. So she was happy to cut the pattern. It was challenging, but it did feel good.

Sharon worked in the mornings and studied English, maths, and word processing in the afternoons. The English teacher was a very down-to-earth, kindly man in his sixties named Ken. Sharon enjoyed this class because Ken was always happy to have an intelligent discussion on most topics, from history, geography, and different cultures to points of the daily news. Ken never treated the girls as prisoners. To him, they were students, and he never asked them why they were there. When Sharon left prison, she sent him her best regards and many thanks.

The prisoners didn't work Friday afternoons or weekends. They were locked up at 4:45 on weekends. Sharon would get up in the morning to clean her own room. Then she would go to the gym.

The gym was quite large and very well stocked. Sharon would stay there for about two hours.

She had her own room at Morton Hall, but she did have to share the shower and toilet with the other girls. After a prisoner had been in Morton Hall for eight weeks, if she had behaved herself and not gotten into any trouble, she could apply to be moved to another unit, where girls had their own rooms with an en-suite toilet, shower, and sink. This unit was called the Windsor Unit. It was all very modern and clean. So Sharon applied to move there and got accepted. She was delighted by not having to go to a toilet with anyone else.

Sharon moved into Windsor within one week. The officers there were very helpful and pleasant. It didn't really feel like being in prison. It was more like a girls' camp.

There were about four hundred girls in the prison. Three hundred fifty of them were foreign nationals, and only about fifty of them were English. The girls there were very young. Most of the foreign nationals were in for drug trafficking. They'd be picked up at the airports. They got nine-year sentences and then were deported at the end of their sentences and weren't allowed back into England for ten years. Most of the English girls were drug addicts who had been sentenced for burglary, plus GBH or prostitution. Sharon used to see them in the doctor's surgery every morning, waiting for the methadone because they had withdrawal symptoms.

This prison had very strict rules about bullying. If you got caught bullying, you got sent to the segregation unit—no telling in the room, no privileges. If you caused too much trouble, you got shipped out to another prison. One woman was in her early forties, yet she didn't have any teeth. Sharon had never met anyone without any teeth, especially at that age. She must have been a junkie. She had seven children and was in prison for two years for setting fire to her boyfriend's golf clubs. They had been on the landing outside his room in a house he shared with other people.

Morton Hall prisoners were allowed to send out as many letters as they wanted, and they could receive as many back after they had read theirs. They were not allowed hairspray, bleach, scissors, or anything they could harm themselves with.

Some of the officers were quite rude on Saturday mornings; they would come into the rooms to check the security alarms. If you were sitting in your room reading or writing, they would come into the room, check the alarm, look in the wardrobe, look under the bed, and go out without acknowledging that you were sitting there.

IF YOU WANTED TO GO to the gym or library or across the yard to talk to someone, it had to be documented; you could not move without getting written permission.

One evening, a lady called Donna was rushed to hospital on a stretcher. At first, the doctors thought it was her heart, but afterwards, they said it was suspected gallstones. When Donna got back to the prison, she told the girls the prison officers handcuffed her all the time when they took her by stretcher and all the time she was in hospital. When she wanted to go to the toilet, they handcuffed her with a long chain and waited outside the toilet door for her. She was really, really ill. She was sent back to hospital several times before she went home.

The prison officers were mean about turning on the central heating. They wouldn't turn it on until the end of October. In September, it got quite cold, but they still wouldn't turn on the heating. Sharon had to buy a hot water bottle to keep warm. If she wouldn't have had that, she would have been ill.

On Friday 20 2009, Sharon was invited to the launch of a book of short stories written by the girls of Morton Hall. It was to be held in the visiting hall. As attendees entered the hall, all the comfy chairs were lined up in a row. And there was a very nice buffet laid out. Plus, no one searched the girls on this occasion. It made the girls almost forget they were in prison for a short period.

They all took their seats, and the speeches started. First was a woman called C.J., the mentor responsible for the course. Next was the governor, Mr Bennit, who praised the girls for their achievement and said he was really impressed by their efforts. He quoted many different people who had written while in prison, like Nelson Mandela and Anne Frank.

After the speeches finished, about ten girls got up one by one and read a short part of their stories. They were really heart-rending and brought tears to people's eyes. Some of them cried as they were reading. When Sharon saw these ten girls walking around the prison, she had no idea about their backgrounds or what happened that may have contributed to their ending up in prison. This event made Sharon realise that her problem was tiny compared to theirs.

After they finished their introductions, the girls had their photos taken. Then everyone tucked into the refreshments and cake. Sharon felt human just for having a serviette. Normally, when they went to the canteen as part of the daily routine, they had to walk back to their unit with the food stuck on their plastic plates and their dirty knives and forks. It was so demoralising.

She couldn't stop thinking about the confiscation hearing, which was due to take place in September. The judge was going to claim all of Sharon's assets, claiming that all the money that had gone through Sharon's hands over the last ten year was dirty money. The prosecution had engaged a forensic accountant to try to justify this. Sharon knew they wouldn't find anything because she simply didn't earn the sort of money they were talking about; what Sharon earned had mostly gone to the girls and Sharon's family. Sharon didn't actually have any surplus money, not even any savings.

This was the justice system in this country. They wanted to take away the title that Sharon had: just a little equity in her house.

AND AT THE AGE OF 63, Sharon was expected to sell her house and walk the streets like a bag lady. Sharon thought that in her case, the only victim was her. She was a woman in her sixties who'd brought up her family and was a grandmother. She hadn't been in prison for violence, or trafficking, or cruelty to the girls. In fact, she had taken care of the girls and given them a chance to send money home to their mothers and families.

Sharon was really angry when she found out she was classified as a MAPPA on her prison profile. She asked an officer, 'What is a MAPPA?' and the officer answered, 'You don't need to worry about that.'

So Sharon went to the library to read up on what it meant in the Archibald. There, she discovered that MAPPA stands for Multi-Agency Public Protection Arrangement, meaning you are an unsafe person and not to be trusted around young people. So she had been put on the MAPPA register related to sexual offences with violence. Sharon was never violent to anybody, nor did she ever make anybody do anything against their will.

When Sharon got out of jail, she went to an organisation that gives advice to women needing help after prison, and they suggested she write to the head of the prison services regarding her MAPPA status. That's what she did, and she did get a letter back saying they'd made a mistake and they were going to take her off the register. *At least that was put right,* Sharon thought.

After her release, Sharon reported to her probation officer. He was telling her all the things she could and could not do as a MAPPA. She said, 'Just a second. I'm not a MAPPA. I want to take in lodgers in the upstairs of my house to help me pay the mortgage, and I want to do some beauty work.'

He said pompously, 'You can't. You can't have any people in your house.' When she asked why, he said, 'Because they say that you might coerce them into prostitution.'

'But I'm not a MAPPA,' Sharon said. Sharon showed him the letter from prison services, which he took into a back room.

Then he came out and said, 'I'm sorry, Sharon. You are a MAPPA.'

SO AGAIN, SHARON WENT TO the Women's Prison Office on City Road in the city of London. She explained what the probation officer had said, and she agreed she would see to it that they did take her off the MAPPA register. She did get removed eventually, but it did take a lot of hoo-ha. The only thing that Sharon was guilty of was allowing the girls to do what they wanted within reason. It was their choice. For that, she ended up in prison with hardened criminals.

When she was released, she couldn't get house insurance or car insurance because she now had a criminal record. It certainly changed her life. She lost her credit status and her dignity. Not satisfied with that, they intended to take away her house and her car.

On 2 March 2009, Sharon was released from prison. She was given a lift to the train station, a travel warrant, and £60 in cash. The train was to go straight to London, King's Cross Central Station.

Sharon was so happy to be free. She hadn't seen money for several months, and it was great to be in charge of her handbag and purse again and pay for her cup of tea on the train. She was floating on air with relief, but she was afraid to relax too much in case they had made a mistake and they decided to take her back to prison.

Sharon had to say that prison was an experience that had taught her a lot. She felt mentally and physically stronger after it. She had made some friends there who liked her for the person she was, not for what she had or what she had done. They had cried on one another's shoulders and looked out for one another. She would never forget them. Also, she had gotten an education. She had left there with a literacy, numeracy, and word-processing certificate. All in all, Morton Hall was a valuable experience, but now that it was done, Sharon hoped never to go back there again.

When Sharon arrived home, she was pleased that both her son and her daughter were there to greet her. They had cleaned the house and put some food in the fridge. The three of them had a nice cup of tea and smoked salmon and cream cheese on bagels. It was a really good homecoming.

Sharon said sorry to her daughter for the shame she'd put her through, to which her daughter said, 'That's all right, mum.' She was okay about it. But Sharon could only feel guilty for that.

Sharon went to stay with her daughter in Spain about a year later, for no apparent reason. They got into an argument, which went completely out of control. Sharon's daughter started shouting at her, said a lot of horrible things, and at the end of it said, 'If I'm going to be truthful, I couldn't accept all that bad publicity. I couldn't accept any of it. I'm absolutely devastated,' and she let all her feelings out. That was the first time she actually said anything.

Sharon and her daughter are OK now, but the shame caused by the bad publicity is something Sharon can never repair. Her daughter probably suffered a lot more than Sharon did.

When Sharon was running her business, she never thought there would be fallout for her family because they lived in Essex and she lived in North West London and she never expected to get arrested and sent to prison. She ran her business for over ten years. Everybody knew what was going on, but it was quiet and discreet and didn't bother anybody. If Sharon had ever thought she would end up in prison, she would never have done it. Getting to court was what really brought it home to her how wrong it was. Maybe she was naïve because she thought what the girls did in the room stayed in the room. Sharon never thought that it would ever get out.

Sharon remembered the first time she heard the news of the pop star George Michael being found committing homosexual acts in toilets. She thought, *Oh my God, how does someone get past a scandal like that? How do they face their mums and dads, aunties, uncles?* Yet even that didn't seem to be as bad as what happened to Sharon. No one really gives a damn, do they? But unfortunately, people never forget a scandal; that stays with you forever. Think of what happened with President Clinton and that girl. What a scandal that seemed to be, but nobody's taken any real notice of it. All these scandals blow away in the end, though they're never really forgotten.

Sharon thought it was awful that this scandal of hers affected her and her daughter's relationship.

THE FIRST THING SHARON HAD to face once home was the sorting of the mail. You know what it's like after going on holiday for a couple of weeks. Well, imagine being away for seven months.

There was letter after letter saying, 'Why haven't you responded your returned direct debits?' They were getting stronger and stronger, all threatening court proceedings. And the council tax department had actually got the court to issue judgements against her. It took her a couple of weeks to get them into some kind of order, as before she could talk to any of them, she had to wait a week to get the phone put back on.

It was such an ordeal. She might have served only seven out of fifteen months, but when she was let out of prison, it took her another four months to get her house in some kind of order. If that wasn't enough, she had to report to the probation office every week so that they could keep a check on her.

The funny thing was that since Sharon had been home, several of the girls had been to see her, saying they weren't working. They had tried other places, but they couldn't stay there because the owner was too greedy with the money or the place wasn't as clean as they'd been used to. They wished they could come back and work for Sharon, as they were unhappy and had no money. They said they would have come to court on her behalf, but they were afraid because they knew how manipulative the prosecution could be. And because their English wasn't good, they were afraid they might say something wrong.

One of the girls said she read all the detrimental things said about Sharon in the newspapers, and it made her so sad she wrote an email to a newspaper, trying to explain how good Sharon had been to all the girls and that her working conditions were the best to be found anywhere. But the newspaper never printed her letter, even though Sharon looked for it every day.

SHARON HAD JUST WATCHED A programme on the BBC about whether brothels should be legalised. The Women's Institute was questioned, as were Angela Rippon and George McCoy (author of *McCoy's British Massage Parlour Guide*). These people were in favour of brothels' being legalised. The theory was that it would be safer for the girls, and indeed safer all around. If brothels were registered, it would stop girls' being trafficked. The authorities would be able to keep a check on what was going on.

Sharon said after listening to this debate, she had to agree that over the ten years, she had run her place at a very good standard; it was clean, fair, and safe. There were always plenty of people around, so the girls were never at risk of being ill-treated or murdered. There was CCTV so the girls could see who was at the front door. Apart from one girl's being stupid, it had worked. They could also speak to the people on the intercom. If the girls didn't like the sound of them, they didn't let them in.

Sharon always had a good class of clientele. She had gotten to know the customers, quite a lot of whom had been coming ever since the first day she opened. It had become like a second home for a lot of them. Some would come in and make a cup of tea or coffee. Some sat in the garden and had a cigarette with the girls. Some would watch a football match. If Sharon knew a guy who lived on his own and she was cooking, she would invite them to join her for a meal.

Not only was it safe for the girls, but the guys felt incredibly welcome there. Plus, what happened at Sharon's place never interfered with the men's private lives. They knew that once they left, there wouldn't be any comebacks. Many men need what they cannot get at home. It fills in the gaps for them. They knew they weren't going to be ripped off at Sharon's; she only took £20 from the girls, so everyone was getting a fair deal.

SHARON'S PLACE ALWAYS HAD A good selection of girls, so the girls had the freedom of choosing the hours and days they worked. Every man had a preferred type of woman he needed to be with.

Some really young guys wanted quite mature women. They lacked confidence and felt more relaxed with a mother figure who they thought would teach them a thing or two. Then there were really good-looking guys whose wives were prima donnas and would not put themselves out. They thought being loved was their right and their right only. So their husbands needed a lot of TLC.

Then there were women who let themselves go and were very overweight whose husbands were probably yearning for a skinny lady. While some women had small breasts and their husbands may be dying for a buxom woman, there were also very shy men who could not get a girlfriend or men who didn't have enough money to get a girlfriend. Some men just wanted to be massaged.

Sharon's house was very clean. She had a cleaner in every day who thoroughly cleaned with bleach. And the house had clean towels and plenty of clean sheets for the massage couches, and there were showers in all the rooms. She had the washing going all day to make sure they never ran out of towels even though the electricity bill was sky high. Sharon took every care to make sure her house was a happy house. It wasn't a sin to open it. It was a sin to close it.

Since it was closed down, Sharon had many emails and text messages saying the clients never found anywhere else to go where they felt happy and relaxed.

THERE WERE A LOT OF unhappy men walking around, and now, a lot of unhappy ladies because they couldn't work in Sharon's secure, happy surroundings. If the law changed, Sharon would go back into the industry because she knew how to treat people involved in it. Sharon's place had been the best place anywhere, and the law had a lot to answer for. There most certainly hadn't been any trafficking of women nor underage girls or drugs, and nobody had had any problems.

The feedback from the customers was they hadn't had anywhere to go since Sharon's place closed down. They liked Sharon's place because they felt safe there. They went there, had their massage and whatever else, and felt a lot better by the time they left. Sharon didn't exploit anyone and felt that the law should be changed so that brothels were properly controlled by local councils. The councils should issue licences and make regular visits to ensure that nobody was being mistreated or ripped off, no girls were being trafficked, and nobody was being coerced.

At the age of 64, Sharon had to sell her house to give the crown the equity from it. They were not satisfied that they had sent her to prison. Now that she was out, she couldn't even get insurance on her house or car. Plus, she was expected to sell the house for the equity.

The judge said Sharon made money from prostitution. Sharon said she charged only £20 per hour to use the facilities; she thought that was more than fair. Sharon had all the expenses of running the house, paying for advertising and the telephone bills, electricity, and laundry. When the forensic people went through Sharon's transactions, they didn't find any money because there wasn't any. The judge said because the girls charged £50 for a massage, and they gave Sharon £20 out of that, the £20 was money from prostitution. So if Sharon would have had more sense, she should have charged the men £20 as an entry fee to use the house. Then things could have been different. She didn't know the law.

THERE IS A NEED FOR adult services. They take all the stress away, and they do you good. The girls enjoy them too.

Brothels are legal in Germany, Holland, Spain, Australia, and many other countries, and even the Women's Institute is in favour of regulating them. And although they said Sharon's place was a brothel, you could always get a very good therapeutic massage there, and everyone knows the benefits of a good massage.

Lightning Source UK Ltd.
Milton Keynes UK
UKHW010804090721
386819UK00011B/329

9 781665 590662